M

Wild sounds came from the pines above them. Something moving through the forest, knocking into tree trunks, crashing and falling through brushes, coming fast.

"Oh, God, it's a bear," Ruth said.

Ruth grabbed her backpack and madly rifled through it. "A knife. I brought a knife. We'll kill it."

"No," Helma ordered. "Drop to the ground and curl up. Cover the back of your neck with your hands to protect your spine."

But they both stood rooted to the trail. The crashing increased, grew closer, and a shape broke from the trees, stumbling, then falling and rolling down the sloping meadow toward them.

It wasn't a black bear or a grizzly; it was a man . . . and he was covered with blood.

Other Miss Zukas Mysteries by
Jo Dereske
from Avon Books

OUT OF CIRCULATION

A MISS ZUKAS MYSTERY

JO DERESKE

AVON BOOKS NEW YORK

This is a work of fiction. Names, characters, places, and incidents either are the product of the author's imagination or are used fictitiously. Any resemblance to actual events, locales, organizations, or persons, living or dead, is entirely coincidental and beyond the intent of either the author or the publisher.

AVON BOOKS
A division of
The Hearst Corporation
1350 Avenue of the Americas
New York, New York 10019

Inside cover author photo by Teresa Salgado Photography
Published by arrangement with the author
Visit our website at **http://AvonBooks.com**
Library of Congress Catalog Card Number: 97-93011
ISBN: 0-380-78244-8

First Avon Books Printing: September 1997

Printed in the U.S.A.

WCD 10 9 8 7 6 5 4 3 2 1

For K. and Lyssa Keusch

CONTENTS

chapter one

BROKEN PROMISES

On Saturday morning, when Ruth Winthrop accused Miss Helma Zukas of not keeping her word and skipping out on probably the best friend she'd ever have in her entire life, the sun was shining. The September air was crisp and warm, the sky autumn blue, and the waters of Washington Bay lightly riffled and glinted like gems.

The preceding month had been exceptionally warm and sunny, uncharacteristically dry for the Pacific Northwest. The inhabitants of Bellehaven, Washington, unaccustomed to such largess, had determinedly spent every sunny day outside and now sported suntans, outdoor muscles, and a mild irritability brought on by the responsibility of relentless good weather. Sales of sunglasses were way up.

Even Helma Zukas's skin, despite her best efforts, was slightly bronzed, forcing to the surface forgotten freckles she covered with a pale concealer that came in a tube like lipstick.

"Think of it as my birthday present," Ruth, who was the tannest Helma had ever seen her, said, rising from the arm of the chair where she'd been sitting. Ruth's clothing style had recently taken another sharp detour. A month earlier, she'd phoned Helma at eleven o'clock at night to announce her body was sliding down her skeleton and from that instant on, she was retiring from pants, shorts, and leggings, forever and evermore. Which left an array of colorful dresses and skirts brushing ankle or exposing thigh, elongating Ruth's six foot, one inch body to eye-catching proportions, which Helma suspected had been Ruth's intention all along.

Today Ruth wore an orange t-shirt that hung to the hem of a blue skirt, shod in black sneakers without socks, her black hair bushed.

"But Ruth," Helma reminded her as she carefully removed a watercolor of a Skagit Valley tulip field from her apartment wall and dusted its back. "Your birthday isn't until December."

"That's why we have to go *now*," Ruth said, pulling a roll of peppermint Lifesavers from the pocket of her skirt and thumbing three into her mouth. "You can't hike in the mountains in December. You can barely even drive up to the ski area and that's not even halfway up the mountain. It snows big time in the winter up there, remember?"

Helma winced as Ruth stood in front of the sliding glass doors and gazed out over Helma's balcony at the waters of Washington Bay, chewing her Lifesavers with teeth-grinding crunches. "Everybody and his brother has a sailboat," Ruth muttered between chomps. "Look at all of them out there, puffing and luffing. I can't even afford a rowboat."

Helma refrained from mentioning the word "savings." Ruth's economic philosophy was simple: when her paintings sold well, she spent her money until it was gone and then unconcernedly lived on boiled eggs, cornflakes, and the kindness of friends until her fortunes turned.

"I'm aware it snows in the mountains," Helma assured Ruth as she rehung the watercolor over the circle of mishammered holes in her wall. "But I don't understand the urgency to hike *now*."

"Because I *want* to," Ruth said. She turned and squinted at Helma, her eyes narrowing. "You're *afraid* to hike in the mountains, aren't you? Up where it's all wild and unorganized, dirty even?"

"I certainly am not." Helma flicked a piece of lint off her pants even though she was dressed in her cleaning clothes: a faded pair of jeans she'd first donned for a high school canoe trip over twenty years ago and a blue t-shirt that read across the front, "Love your Library," with a stylized heart replacing the word "love."

"Are too. When's the last time you went hiking, I mean *really* hiking?"

"I hike," Helma protested. She stepped back and critically eyed the watercolor: yellow and red rows of tulips marching toward the mountains like distant railroad tracks. She closed one eye and peered over her hand, which she held first perfectly parallel, then perfectly perpendicular to her ceiling. Straight. "Every day."

"You *walk*," Ruth corrected with a touch of disdain. "Over flat land on little paved trails through our little civilized town. That's a weaker breed of animal than charging up a remote mountainside in the shadow of old growth forests, the basic necessities of life on your back, surviving by vestigial instincts, surrounded by the calls of the wild." Ruth closed her eyes, contemplating the wonder of it all.

A few weeks earlier, Ruth, who drove from one end of the mall to the other rather than walk its length, had participated in a brief affair with a younger man from Seattle who wrote trail guides illustrated by cartoon figures and filled with rock music lyrics and quotes from Henry David Thoreau. She'd accompanied him on a single mountain hike, "carrying his pencil," she'd told Helma, and now considered herself a woman with experience in the higher elevations.

"My walks have every characteristic of hiking," Helma said. "The elevation of Bellehaven varies between sea level and 641 feet. That hardly qualifies as 'flat' terrain."

"Helma," Ruth said, twisting the drapery cord around her finger. "Do you know what birthday this is?"

"Your fortieth," Helma told her.

"I didn't ask you to *say* it." Ruth wrapped the cord around her neck and pretended to hang herself. "And don't tell me it's better than the alternative."

"It is," Helma said. "But what does your fortieth birthday have to do with a hike in the mountains? You're treating it like an emergency."

Ruth grabbed hold of her right thigh with both hands and jiggled her flesh. "*This* is an emergency. And *this*," poking her upper arm. "Time. Time is passing at an ever more alarming rate. Forget the endangered species; I need to save what *I* have left. Once it's gone, it's gone."

"It might be more appropriate to join a gym," Helma suggested as she removed an oil painting of a sailboat moving sedately through calm seas.

Ruth guffawed. "All that regimental sweat? No thanks. Besides, climbing up a mountain is more beneficial than one of those stair-climbing machines. What do you say?"

"About gyms?" Helma asked.

"About taking a mountain hike with me? It'll be step one of getting back in shape. I'm thinking of taking up jogging, too, maybe dance. Or yoga." She looked at her reflection in the glass, smoothing her chin line with the fingertips of both hands. "I'll greet the new decade looking like a twenty-year-old. You can, too."

"I'm not out of shape," Helma said. And that was

true. She faithfully exercised for forty-five minutes three times a week and walked every day, rain or shine, good mood or not, and was still the same size she'd been in high school. Even her hair was curled in the same becoming style she'd worn in high school.

"So great," Ruth said. "Then you won't be lagging behind me up the trails."

"Ruth . . ." Helma began.

Ruth placed her hands on her hips. "Have you ever, *ever* in your entire life, hiked in the mountains with a backpack on your shoulders?" she demanded.

"I've driven into the mountains as far as the road allows," Helma told her, glancing around her walls to be sure every painting was straight and true.

"Hah! I didn't think so. Do you want to die without experiencing the mountains up close and personal, pine-scented air that hasn't been overbreathed, marmots frolicking in the rocks? You might as well go back to Michigan."

"It isn't necessary to spend days in the mountains in order to appreciate them," Helma explained.

Ruth smiled in small triumph and sat on the arm of Helma's couch, swinging her leg. "Okay, no *days* in the mountains; so how about *one* day? Think of it: just one short day."

"One day where?" Helma asked warily, folding her dustcloth into a square and returning it to her portable cleaning caddy.

"Where?" Ruth repeated, then shrugged and pointed east, over her shoulder, through Helma's walls and behind Bellehaven where the gentle land mounded into green, tree-covered foothills and then soared into the snow-covered mountain range capped by Mount Baker. "Up."

"You're speaking of thousands of square miles, Ruth. A more specific destination would be helpful."

"We'll look one up," Ruth said brightly. "Dougie left me one of his hiking books and you have a zillion in the library." When Helma looked doubtful, Ruth cajoled, "It'll be fun, it'll be gorgeous. This has been the driest and warmest summer in years, everybody says so. No creeks to cross, no muck. Even the bomber's out," Ruth said, expressing it the way Northwesterners did when Mount Baker or Mount Rainier was visible: the mountain's out.

Helma knew the bomber was out. Its periodic sighting created a flurry of excitement similar to an announcement of the elusive apparition some claimed haunted the city museum's staircase.

During the World War II years, a squadron of Lockheed PV-1 bombers conducting maneuvers over the state was caught in an unexpected early snowstorm. One PV-1 vanished from the squadron, without a single radio transmission, and fears were that the plane had strayed into the dangerous mountain range, but no trace of the missing plane was found.

Thirty years later, during another exceptionally warm summer in the 1970's, the melting snow had receded enough to partially uncover the crash site and a group of climbers had stumbled upon the downed bomber at the edge of a glacier, solving that decades-old mystery.

Human traces were removed but the well-preserved remains of the PV-1 were left behind, covered year round by ten and twenty feet—or more—of snow, briefly reappearing every few years when abnormal summers melted the plane's snowy shroud. Only the most experienced hikers and climbers dared brave the rough terrain to the crash site.

"I'm not prepared to hike to the bomber," Helma said.

"No," Ruth assured her. "We'll find a trail that's as

easy as pie. Just zip up the mountains and down again. Work our bodies into sleek machines.'' Ruth snapped her fingers. ''It'll be a piece of cake. What could go wrong?''

chapter two

UNREST IN THE RANKS

Before Helma left her apartment in the Bayside Arms for the Bellehaven Public Library on Monday morning, she tended to Boy Cat Zukas, whose life and well-being she'd reluctantly but officially taken responsibility for the previous winter. A metal tag hung from a collar around his neck to prove it.

Boy Cat Zukas's appearance was much improved since Helma took command. The black alley cat's pelt shone; the bare patches had healed, his new hair growing in white. His torn ear had been resewn, and his diet was now scientifically designed for the mature male cat of the species. A groomer picked up Boy Cat Zukas on the third Monday of every month for a flea bath and claw trimming, an ordeal from which Helma would have expected Boy Cat Zukas to flee, but instead he broached no protest when the groomer appeared, even climbing into the cat carrier without prompting. He now slept inside Helma's apartment, beside her balcony door in a wicker cat basket plumped with a red cushion Helma put through her washing machine and dryer every Saturday morning.

Boy Cat Zukas showed no particular gratitude for the

beneficial effects of Helma's ownership but as long as he kept his distance, Helma was satisfied with their wary coexistence. She'd never touched the cat and, as if by mutual consent, the two maintained a respectful, if suspicious, attentiveness toward one another.

Geraniums, daisies, and petunias still bloomed in clay pots on Helma's balcony, their lives extended by the continuing summerlike weather. Helma slid open the balcony door and Boy Cat Zukas slipped outside, flicking his tail. He swiped at a pink geranium blossom, scattering petals on the decking, before nonchalantly jumping on the balcony railing and from there to the third-story roof, beginning his mysterious daily rounds.

Another sunny day. Already the humps of the San Juan Islands were pinpointed by sunlight, and the western reaches of the bay glistened as if a spotlight had been turned on the placid water. To the north, the Canadian mountains glowed in purple haze. Two seagulls wheeled above the apartment building, squawking shrilly, followed immediately by Boy Cat Zukas's irritated meow from the roof.

A sailboat passed the Bayside Arms, its sails lowered in the calm morning, motoring toward the mouth of the bay. Helma pulled her opaque window shades on the scene, checked her hair in the mirror beside the door, and departed for work.

She braked her car at the parking lot exit, waiting for a bevy of young girls to giggle past on their way to the closest middle school. School had begun three days ago and students were still eager, leaving home with time to spare, their clothing crisp with newness, their faces bright with anticipation. In another week they'd begin trudging into the library, homework orders in hand, anticipation turned to sullen impatience.

But Helma preferred the most sullen of students to the desperate, stressed-out parents who materialized later in the school year, sweating over their child's homework while Johnny or Suzie tended to soccer or piano lessons.

As Helma pulled into her space in the Bellehaven Public Library's too-small parking lot, aligning the center of her Buick's hood with the flagpole, she was surprised to see the knot of library employees standing outside on the loading dock at the rear of the library.

Had the library been evacuated in an emergency? She studied the building for signs of billowing smoke or grave-faced policemen. But no, the brick library was serene and whole and as Helma stepped from her Buick, she more closely examined the little group standing where the bookmobile normally loaded and unloaded.

Gray-haired Mrs. Carmon, the plump circulation clerk who was counting down the days until her retirement, stood facing a stern assembly of fifteen to twenty employees, her face flushed, her grandmotherly countenance steely.

Whatever had been transpiring, the gathering stood silently—Helma thought self-consciously, maybe even guiltily—as she approached the rear entrance to the library.

No librarians stood on the loading dock, only clerks and staff assistants, a few pages, lips pursed and eyes averted. Junie, the cataloging clerk, gave a tiny, hands-down wave as Helma passed the group before she entered the staff door into the crowded library workroom.

George Melville, the cataloging librarian, looked up from his cataloging corner where his computer screen displayed a colorful game of Hearts and jerked a thumb over his shoulder toward the door. "Have they begun rioting yet? Do we have time to boil the oil and bar the doors?"

"Why are they holding a meeting on the loading dock?" Helma asked.

George scratched his chin through his beard and put a finger to his lips. "You've just witnessed a budding insurrection. Care to see what I caught Junie making when she was supposed to be sticking bar codes on book covers?'' And he reached behind a stack of books and pulled out a poster-sized placard.

''Ta da!'' he said and turned it toward Helma. Not all the letters were filled in by purple ink but the message clearly read: I'M NOT UN-PROFESSIONAL; I'M A PROFESSIONAL PARAPROFESSIONAL.

''I don't understand,'' Helma said, admiring Junie's evenly spaced and well-lettered message. A professional sign painter couldn't have done a better job.

''You know how the Moonbeam likes to separate 'professional' ''—here George made quotation marks in the air with wagging fingers—''librarians from 'nonprofessional' staff members.''

Helma herself never would have called Ms. Moon ''the Moonbeam'' but she knew what George was talking about. The director was fierce in protecting the territory of librarians who held Masters degrees from the inroads of staff members who might have the knowledge but lacked the pedigree.

''Royalty and peasant,'' George Melville went on. ''Prom queen and court. Diva and chorus. Doctors and nurses.'' His eyes went distant and Helma interrupted him before he could favor her with new analogies.

''Are you saying the staff is intending to *demonstrate* against being called the 'nonprofessional' staff?'' she asked, holding up Junie's placard.

''You got it,'' George said, pointing his coffee cup at her. ''Mrs. Carmon, our loyal circulation clerk, sees retirement looming on the horizon and hopes to belatedly make her mark, so she's assumed leadership of the pack. They're demanding a new designation.''

''Which is?''

George shrugged. ''I'm afraid to ask.''

''Are they requesting higher wages as well?''

"No, just new names. Oh, and the right to attend library conferences." He shook his head. "Now *there's* a misguided request, if there ever was one. I'll gladly relinquish my attendance rights. Heck, I'll *pay* somebody to go in my place."

If Helma were going to all that effort just to protest a designation as innocuous as "nonprofessional," she'd certainly include a request for more money as well. It seemed the most efficient thing to do.

Harley Woodworth was already seated at his desk in his cubicle next to Helma's, taking his own blood pressure. His ears were plugged by the ear tips of a stethoscope so Helma was able to slip her purse into her desk drawer and leave her cubicle for the public area without having to engage in conversation with the health-absorbed librarian.

The library didn't open for two more hours and since the staff members who usually reshelved books and prepared for each new day were now busy plotting rebellion on the loading dock, the public area was empty: silent and shadowed. Helma turned on the lights above the nonfiction stacks and made her way to the 790's, where the hiking books were shelved.

She chose six, ranging from *Take a Hike!* to the more advanced: *The Professional Hiker; Rules of the Trail,* and carried them to her desk.

"One-thirty-six over eighty-three," Harley Woodworth reported as Helma entered her cubicle. "Edging up."

Helma pretended not to hear Harley's daily announcement, averting her eyes from Harley's cubicle with its colorful "Dangerous Moles" poster, medical textbooks, reams of health advice printed off the Internet, and rows of vitamin bottles.

"One-thirty-six over eighty-three," he repeated in a louder voice, rising and peering over the low bookshelves that separated his work cubicle from Helma's.

Harley Woodworth was young, only six years out of graduate school and the holder of five brief professional jobs since obtaining his library degree, which instead of alarming Ms. Moon, had inspired her to hire Harley as a kind of vocational project: the rescue of a professional colleague for the greater good of librarianship.

Harley was long-jawed and thin. He buttoned the top button of his shirts and always wore a wide brown belt sporting a chrome buckle engraved with his initials: HAW, for Harley Arlan Woodworth, and who George Melville referred to as "Hardly Worthit."

"One-thirty-six over eighty-three," he repeated, ominously this time.

"Congratulations," Helma told him.

"Yesterday it was one-twenty-seven over eighty-one. The lower number is more important, you know. It's rising."

"You're well below the danger level," Helma assured him. "Now if you'll excuse me."

"Danger is a relative term," Harley said. "I can take yours, too," he offered, holding up the gray cuff.

"No, thank you."

Harley leaned across the bookshelf barrier and tapped her stack of hiking books with a long finger.

"Are you planning a hiking trip?"

"I'm conducting research for a friend," Helma told him.

"My cousin knew somebody who took up hiking," he said. "Went into Glacier Park." He paused, his voice on the upbeat.

"And?" Helma asked, immediately chastising herself for encouraging Harley, whose tales invariably ran to bad ends.

"From the size of the bite marks, they figured it was an eight-foot grizzly. There wasn't much left. You never know.'' He shook his head knowledgeably, opened his jaws without parting his lips, and disappeared behind his side of the shelves.

Helma quickly perused the hiking books, eliminating *Happy Trails* and a volume on high meadow meditation before setting aside the remaining four to check out.

Despite what Ruth claimed, Helma considered her daily walks to be as good as hikes. She didn't camp; she hadn't slept on bare ground since that one night in her backyard when she was eleven years old. That adventure had been aborted after her cousin Ricky used a stolen cigarette lighter to set fire to her tent. And it was true: she hadn't spent time in any forest beyond the trees of a well-tended park since her childhood, either, although she *could* recognize and identify seventeen different species of tree.

But now that Ruth had agreed to a simple hike, an afternoon's vigorous exercise in the mountains, Helma was almost looking forward to the adventure. No sleeping on dirt or cooking over unpredictable campfires. Maybe Ruth really did mean it: this was step one to a healthier lifestyle.

''Did you hear about the bomb yesterday?'' George Melville asked as he passed Helma's desk on his way from the staff lounge, carrying a coffee cup the size of a soup bowl.

''At the park?'' Helma asked.

''Only bomb I know of. Blew a hole in the men's restroom that you could drive a bicycle through.''

''A Hole in One!'' the headline in last night's *Bellehaven Daily News* had read.

''Have they caught whoever was responsible?'' Helma asked.

George shook his head. ''Nope. Kids on a prank, I'll bet.''

Helma had missed the explosion itself in the park that

edged Washington Bay, but she'd seen the flashing lights and heard the sirens.

"Did your chief of police spill any of the details?" George asked, leaning closer into Helma's cubicle.

"I haven't spoken to him recently," Helma said.

George raised his eyebrows and shrugged his shoulders as if he were freezing. "The air's still frigid between you two, eh?" he asked.

"Be careful," Helma warned him. "You'll spill your coffee."

George winked and walked away, saying, "I hear you loud and clear," while Helma restacked the hiking books by size, feeling her face flush.

She turned as the workroom door slammed and the disgruntled staff members entered from the loading dock, single file, heads high, stout Mrs. Carmon leading the way. Grim silence accompanied their passage. In the cubicle on the other side of Helma's, Eve, the fiction librarian, stood and watched the somber procession, twisting a yellow curl around her finger. "Do you think they'll go on strike?" she asked Helma in a whisper.

"Of course not. If all they're demanding is a change in their job titles, Ms. Moon will agree to that."

Eve raised her eyebrows and glanced toward the director's dimly lit office, where Ms. Moon sat at her desk with her eyes closed, a slight smile on her face. The director's door was open as always, barely audible sitar music issuing forth.

When Helma reported to the reference desk in the public area to relieve Harley Woodworth of his reference duties and begin her own three-hour stint on the desk, she arrived in time to see Harley holding a Chilton's motor repair manual to his chest and telling the young man in mechanic's clothing in front of him, "This is a library book. Look at your fingernails."

The young man took an uncertain step backward, his face flaming red. Helma leaned between the two men, saying "Excuse me," to Harley and removing the Chilton's manual from his hands with a meaningful tug. She then smiled and presented it to the young mechanic.

"Don't worry," she told him. "We *expect* these manuals to come back greasy. That's why we have several copies, so they'll be used."

"Thanks," the young man told Helma, shooting a dark glance at Harley.

"Germs," Harley said as the mechanic walked toward the circulation desk, the thick manual cradled in his arm. "And dirt."

"He's a taxpayer," Helma told Harley. "He pays your salary. Now if you'll remove your belongings from the desk, it appears to be a very busy morning."

An hour later, a phone call from Ruth made it through to the congested reference desk. "It's all set," Ruth sang out in Helma's ear.

Four people stood in front of Helma, awaiting her attention, another call was blinking on the telephone, and she had yet to deal with a woman who'd snuck her Chihuahua into the library inside her purse.

"What's all set?" Helma asked as she handed the first man in line the *World Almanac*, pointing to the population of Mali.

"Our hiking trip, did you forget already?"

"I'm very busy right now, Ruth," Helma said, beckoning the next person forward, a woman holding a potted plant with glossy leaves that brushed her chin.

"That's what the clerk who answered told me. What's going on down there? She told me, 'Our *professional* librarians are too busy to take your call but may *I* help you?' I told her to cut the crap and put you on the line."

Helma leaned back in her chair and looked over at the staff manning the circulation desk. Mrs. Carmon was checking out a two-foot tall pile of books for a patron and glanced over at Helma, defiantly raising her chin.

"But about our hiking trip," Ruth continued. "You don't have to worry about a thing. We're set for next Wednesday. These people I know, Bill and Ariel Butler, are going with us; they know *everything* about hiking. A three-day trip, okay? I'll be over at exactly six o'clock to give you the details, six-fifteen tops," she said, and hung up while Helma was exclaiming, "A *three-day* trip?"

chapter three

SCATTERED TRAILS

When Helma arrived home after work, the plumber was still in her apartment, lying on his back beneath her kitchen sink like a ''Dagwood'' cartoon, his head and upper body invisible. On the floor sat her cleaning caddy and all her cleaning supplies.

Walter David, the manager of the Bayside Arms, leaned against her kitchen counter, reading Helma's copy of the *Bellehaven Daily News.* He greeted her with a wide smile when she walked in.

The drain trap beneath her sink had leaked a week ago and this was the earliest the manager could book a plumber. At the time, Helma had used a wrench from the tool kit her mother had given her for Christmas, temporarily stopping the leak herself.

''Hope you don't mind,'' the chunky landlord told Helma. He shook the newspaper. ''This was on the mat so I brought it in for you while I waited for the plumber to finish. They haven't caught the guys who bombed that restroom yet, I see,'' he said, holding the front page toward her. ''I'd be careful walking down at the park every day if I were you.''

"Oh damn," the plumber mumbled from beneath the sink.

"Trouble?" Walter David asked, leaning over and raising his voice as if the plumber were in the next room, not directly beneath his feet.

"Somebody ratcheted this until they stripped the threads," the plumber told him tersely.

"Tough break," Walter said. He turned to Helma. "Where's Boy Cat?"

"He'll probably appear at the balcony door any minute," Helma told him, setting her bag and purse on the kitchen table.

Walter David loved cats. He'd even built a seat on the back of his Harley-Davidson for Moggy, his Persian. Last winter, after Walter had resigned himself to the fact that Boy Cat Zukas, the alley cat, was responsible for purebred Moggy's pregnancy, and Moggy had birthed a litter of mongrel kittens, Walter had banged on every apartment door in the building at eleven-thirty at night to share the good news. When Helma, who didn't answer her door after 9 p.m., hadn't responded, he'd phoned her, letting it ring until she answered.

In Helma's opinion, the features of Moggy's four kittens were much improved by Boy Cat Zukas's gene contribution in his final act of fatherhood. To her surprise, the kittens were all spoken for before they were a week old.

After a few more grunts and bangs, the plumber finally finished and emerged from beneath the sink: a youngish man with a broad nose and deep brown eyes. He wiped his hands on the pants of his coveralls and, without looking at Helma, said, "Want me to put this stuff away?"

"No, no," Helma said quickly, glancing at the ousted cleaning supplies. "I'll take care of it."

"Yeah, okay, sure," he said, still not looking at her,

hastily picking up his tools and heading for the door. ''Can you pay me now?'' he asked Walter David.

Walter looked at Helma and shrugged his shoulders, following the plumber out the door. ''Sure.''

Six-fifteen tops, Ruth had said. At six-thirty, Helma turned on her television to the Seattle news station while she waited for Ruth. Boy Cat Zukas crouched outside Helma's balcony door, meowing. Each time Helma unlocked and slid open the screen door, he backed away to the balcony railing and refused to come in, only to return to the door, stridently meowing, the instant she reclosed the screen. ''Oh, Faulkner,'' she said.

The sun still hung brightly in the blue, blue sky and the sound of laughter and voices wafted up from the nearby park and boats on the calm bay.

''News at six-thirty up next,'' a sonorous TV voice announced. ''And here are our top stories: Sunny days continue. Department of transportation names Seattle freeways the third most congested in the nation, and police are investigating a vitamin pyramid scheme that bilked Northwest citizens out of millions of dollars.''

Helma absently reached for the phone to call her mother and remembered that her mother was still in Michigan confronting Aunt Em. Hostilities had never been openly declared but it was a very old, very cold war, beginning, Helma suspected, over forty years ago when her mother had casually eloped with Aunt Em's favorite little brother.

Aunt Em had phoned Helma's mother three weeks ago and declared in her thick Lithuanian accent, ''I'm going to be eighty-six now and that's too old for fighting.'' And then Aunt Em, who loved western movies and who'd learned to operate a VCR just so she could watch old John Wayne videos, had said, ''You come here to duke this out so I can die in peace.''

Helma had watched as her mother—girded for battle—

boarded the little plane at the Bellehaven airport, chin high, armed with Aunt Em's birthday present of smoked salmon tied with a blue bow, and a quiver of grudges. Since then, there'd been silence from across the country, which Helma took as an auspicious sign that peace negotiations were proceeding successfully.

The doorbell jangled and Helma unlocked the door to Ruth, who stood on the doorstep wearing a purple sleeveless dress decorated with what looked like tiny atomic mushroom clouds. She thrust forward a book opened to a turn-of-the-century sepia photograph of men and women hiking on snowy Mount Baker, all in single file, roped waist to waist. "Look at this," Ruth said. "Women used to hike in dresses. Where can I get an outfit like this?"

"The museum?" Helma suggested.

"Ha ha," Ruth deadpanned.

"Surely you can abandon your 'skirts-only' creed for a day, can't you?"

Ruth closed the book. "That would be the first step down the slippery slope. No, I've made up my mind. If I can't wear skirts, I won't go. Besides, dear friend, we're talking three days, not one."

"Ruth, I agreed to a mountain hike, reluctantly if you'll recall, not a three-day camp-out."

Ruth dropped the book on Helma's coffee table and walked across the room to open the screen door for Boy Cat Zukas, who still sat on the balcony, meowing.

"He's been doing that all evening," Helma told her. "He won't come in."

Even before the words were out of Helma's mouth, the black cat padded inside through the open door and curled in his basket, his purrs audible across the room.

"Wilhelmina Zukas," Ruth said fervently, closing the screen door and extending her hands in entreaty. "This is a once-in-a-lifetime opportunity. You're agreeing to a hike to celebrate the deadliest birthday of my life, remember? It's my body-saving kick-off, the first big change in my lifestyle. Momentous.'' She blew a fanfare on an invisible trumpet.

''One day, you said,'' Helma reminded her stubbornly, sitting in her rocker.

Ruth slouched on Helma's couch. ''Think of it,'' she coaxed, her voice dropping dreamily. ''We can hike all the way to Jekyll Glacier; do you understand how rare *that* is? We're talking over six thousand feet *up*. That's almost a mile high.''

''Actually, it's seven hundred and twenty feet higher than a mile,'' Helma told her.

''How'd you know that?''

''Elementary school.''

''No kidding? Anyway, Bill and Ariel are experts, professionals, the top-of-the-line model hikers, so experienced you'll think you're walking through Bellehaven. It'll be fun.''

''Do you know where Jekyll Glacier is?'' Helma asked.

''No, but they do, and Lester at the Sports Corral? He says it's a must-see. It could be gone next time we have a year like this.''

''Glaciers exist for thousands of years,'' Helma told her. She picked up Ruth's book from the coffee table, titled *Northwest Adventures*. It was a library book, a month overdue.

''Yeah, but we don't. Besides, there's this ledge along the trail to Jekyll Glacier called Sky High Overlook. It's supposed to have views to die for. I'm going to take pictures for a new series of paintings.''

''Ruth, I've never known you to paint . . . landscapes.'' Actually, Helma had never deciphered any recognizable representation in any of Ruth's paintings. Only spills of bright pigment, colors that didn't exist in

Helma's apartment or anything she owned.

"*My* version of landscapes," Ruth said, a touch defensively. "You're gonna love 'em. They'll sell like hot cakes." She smiled in anticipation. "And don't forget my opening this Thursday at Bread Biscuit Gallery. This is totally new stuff." Ruth's eyes gleamed dangerously. "I'm going to fix them good."

"Fix who?" Helma asked.

"You'll see. Just be there." When Ruth smiled like that, Helma always found it wiser to be somewhere distant. "So what do you say?" she asked Helma. "Will you go?"

"This couple, Bill and . . ."

"Ariel."

"Bill and Ariel," Helma repeated. "They're experienced?"

"Very very very. They'll meet us at Hyde Point and hike with us to Sky High Overlook. We'll come back down alone while they head toward the glacier to do some ice climbing. See how easy?"

"I can't request vacation time on such short notice."

Ruth leaned forward, pointing her finger at Helma like a gun. "Helma, you can do anything. Just tell the Moon Pie you're on a quest for the cosmic apex of the earth or something."

When Helma still hesitated, Ruth said, "This weather can't last forever. What we have here is a window of opportunity."

"I lack the proper equipment," Helma tried, glancing at a photograph of two early mountain climbers, burdened by wood and canvas backpacks.

"Buy it or rent it at the Sports Corral. Just tell Lester where we're going and he'll fix you right up."

"Do *you* have camping gear?"

"Dougie left me some, I think. If not, I'll borrow somebody else's." Ruth waved toward a vase of bright flowers sitting on Helma's dining room table. ''Who sent you those? Oh, never mind, I know. Our valiant chief of police is still pursuing you, huh? When are you going to give the poor guy a break?''

''He hasn't amended his statement that he prefers we remain friends only,'' Helma told Ruth.

''Give him a sign, idiot. You are one hard case.'' She went to the vase and pulled out a carnation, shoving it behind her ear. ''Speaking of hard cases, do you know that little guy who paints all the whale and dolphin murals around town? With a leprechaunish look?''

''He rides a bicycle?'' Helma asked, rearranging the flowers to make up for the missing carnation.

''Right, with wire baskets on the front and back. Goes by one name, like the guy who sledgehammers watermelons. Bradshaw, I think.''

''I recognize him but I'm not acquainted with him personally.'' She set Ruth's overdue library book on her coffee table and covered it with a *Time* magazine, intending to return it to the library herself.

''Well, neither am I. But he's taken a fancy to yours truly. Rides up and down my alley, just 'happens' to be in the coffee shop or the grocery store when I am. Grinning and scraping and tugging his forelock. It almost gives me the creeps.''

''If you suspect he's following you, talk to the police,'' Helma recommended.

''I don't *know* he's following me.'' Ruth frowned and bit her lip. ''Maybe if he was taller . . . But he's the moony-eyed type, ogling me like a strawberry cheesecake, know what I mean?''

''Not really,'' Helma said.

''Why do I attract those types and let the good ones get away?'' she asked with a touch of melancholy, slumping onto the sofa.

Ruth was referring to Paul from Minneapolis, an ill-fated long-distance relationship that had ended months ago but which shadowed Ruth's current affairs like the wistful memories of an octogenerian's first romance.

"Have you heard from Paul?" Helma asked.

Ruth shrugged and gazed at her hands. "Not really. *Que será, será,* as they say in the movies."

"That was actually a line in a song, not a movie," Helma said. Outside, a starling landed on her balcony railing. Boy Cat Zukas glanced at it, flicked his tail, and yawned.

"The song was *in* an old movie. I saw it on TV when I was little."

"But the words were sung, not said."

"Details," Ruth said, flicking her hand. "So we're set for next Wednesday morning? Seven a.m. sharp. Well, make it eight-thirty. Pick me up. Bill and Ariel are coming up from the south so we'll catch up with them at Hyde Point at four o'clock."

"If I can have the time off, plus accumulate all the equipment."

"Fantastic!" Ruth leaned over, pulled Boy Cat Zukas from his bed by his front legs and kissed him between the eyes, then dropped him unceremoniously to the floor. Boy Cat Zukas wound once around Ruth's legs, purring, then returned to his bed to curl in feline contentment.

Helma's doorbell rang at eight-thirty that evening. She set down her book explaining the proper arrangement of items in a backpack, marking her place with a paper napkin. When she peered through the peep hole she recognized the distorted face of Bellehaven's chief of police, Wayne Gallant, and tucked the stubborn curl behind her ear before she opened the door.

"Helma," he said, nodding, smiling down at her. "I'm sorry to come by so late. Can I talk to you for a minute?"

She stepped back and held the door for him. Wayne Gallant wore a suit with his tie loosened; a lock of his dark hair hung over his forehead. He took Helma's hand as if he were going to shake it and then only held it while she awkwardly tried to pump his hand up and down and finally he gave a short laugh and shook hers, too.

"Would you like a cup of coffee?" she asked. "I have instant."

"No thanks." He ran a big hand through his hair and moistened his lips. "This is a business call, actually."

"What kind of business?" Helma asked.

"Police."

Helma felt her heart thump. "Has anything happened? My mother . . ."

He hurriedly shook his head, holding up his hand. "Oh no, nothing like that. You heard about the bomb in the park's restroom?"

"I did. I read about it in the paper. Have you found the guilty party?"

Wayne Gallant looked up at her overhead light and gave a slight shake of his head. "This is embarrassing," he said to the ceiling.

"I don't understand," Helma told him. She'd never seen him look so uncomfortable, except perhaps that night over dinner several months ago when he'd told her he thought they should just be friends, that he was still raw from his divorce and he was afraid he might get in the way of her developing other "meaningful" relationships.

"Would you mind if I took a peek under your kitchen sink?" He put both hands in his pockets, jingling his keys. "It's just a formality."

"If you need to, go ahead," Helma invited him. "But may I ask why?"

Wayne Gallant opened the cabinet doors beneath her

kitchen sink, pulled at his pant legs, and squatted down. "You had a plumber here tonight?"

"Yes. Was he a criminal?"

He gave her a pained expression, then began sorting through her cleaning supplies. "He called our office after he fixed your drain, claiming you kept enough cleaning supplies under your sink to manufacture a bomb."

"A bomb?" Helma asked. "Why . . . Oh." She gasped. "He thought *I* bombed the men's restroom at the park?"

"I told him I'd check it out." He closed the cabinet doors and raised himself to standing, smiling that smile that crinkled the edges of his eyes, and said, "So now I've checked. I'd say you're clean, I mean, so to speak."

Helma shook her head and sat down at her dining room table, for the tiniest second thrilled that the plumber had suspected she was a bomber, a dangerous woman who whipped up explosives in her kitchen sink. Although she *was* surprised that the plumber believed she'd hide a bomb in a men's restroom.

Wayne Gallant sat down opposite her and scribbled a few lines in his notebook. It always astonished Helma how much space he filled when he was in her apartment, as if all her furniture, and even the size of her rooms, had somehow shrunk.

"How have you been?" he asked as he tucked the notebook back in his pocket.

"Fine. And you?"

"Fine." He nodded, rocking a little in his chair. "Just fine."

The silence in Helma's apartment felt so . . . loud. She glanced over at Boy Cat Zukas, who was in his basket, watching them with one open gold eye.

"I see you got the flowers okay," the chief said, nodding toward the vase on the table.

"Oh yes. Thank you. I dropped you a note, to say

thank you, but you probably haven't received it yet. I put it in today's mail."

"Not yet," he said. He pulled a carnation from the vase, just like Ruth had, but instead of tucking it behind his ear, he twirled it by the stem between his palms. "So you're fine," he said.

"Yes. Everything's fine."

"Glad to hear it." He returned the carnation to the vase, too far to the side, cleared his throat, and said, "Would you like to go out to dinner next Friday?"

"I would," Helma said and then remembered. "But I'll be on a hiking trip."

His blue eyes widened and he studied her for a moment. "You're going hiking?"

"In the mountains," she told him. Then she added, "For three days. With a backpack, and a sleeping bag, all the essentials."

"Perfect weather for it," he said. "Have a good time."

"Thank you." She watched him absently roll the edges of the placemat in front of him and said, "Maybe when I return?"

He smiled at her, leaning forward, and Helma swallowed. "Fine," he said. "That would be fine."

"Fine," she agreed.

On Thursday evening, Helma arrived early at the Bread Biscuit Gallery for Ruth's opening, while Conrad, the gallery owner, was still setting up a table for wine and hors d'oeuvres.

Ruth, dressed in magenta from head to toe, turban to slingbacks, strolled the length of the gallery, a tumblerful of wine in her hand, smiling fondly at her paintings all hung on the bright white walls.

"Take a gander," she said when she saw Helma enter the gallery, waving her glass toward her paintings. "What do you think?"

They were the usual bright slashes and shapes, but in the center of the longest wall hung a row of paintings that seemed to hold Ruth entranced and Helma knew this was the artwork closest to Ruth's heart, her "getting even."

The series was titled "City Hall," and for the first time, Helma was able to clearly see what Ruth had painted, perhaps too clearly. "Ruth," she asked. "What have you done?"

"Beautiful, aren't they?" she asked lovingly.

For the past several months, Ruth had been fruitlessly fighting City Hall. In desperate need of funds for a new skateboard park, the city had forced all artists and writers to purchase business licenses and pay city taxes. Ruth had loudly and flamboyantly fought the "creative license," to no avail.

And now, hung on the wall for all to see, were the instigators of the creative license law. Ruth had painted grotesques, somehow catching undeniable physical features that branded each painting: unkempt hair, thick ankles, a paunchy slouch, burgeoning bellies.

Helma took a step back. "Ruth," she said. "These are too obvious."

"They're supposed to be," Ruth said calmly. "But have no fear; *they* won't see them."

"How do you know that?" Helma asked, helplessly glancing toward the main door which gallery attendees would be passing through in fifteen minutes.

Ruth took another gulp of wine and waved her glass toward the "City Hall" gallery. "These are *numbers* people, my friend. They don't hang out at galleries or read books; they sit in their little dark rooms and play with their digits.''

Helma didn't say anything more but she sincerely hoped that Ruth wouldn't be needing any special favors from the city of Bellehaven in the near future.

chapter four

LATE BEGINNINGS

Helma held two lined sheets of paper bearing a list she'd distilled from her four hiking books as she browsed through the aisles in the Sports Corral, studying prices and thinking that for what this three-day hike was about to cost her, she could afford a pleasant vacation in a distant land.

The young man who volunteered to help her whistled between his teeth when he saw her list. "Everything on this list, please," Helma told him. "Neither the top of the line nor the bottom, just moderately priced and serviceable, for one use."

"We have a larger selection of internal frame packs than external," he told her, pointing to item number one. "They're more popular."

Helma had done her research. "I prefer an external frame to keep the fabric away from my body," she told him. "Less chafing."

BIG SALE BEGINS TUESDAY! a sign with red two-foot-high letters read in the window.

"I intend to buy all my camping gear here," Helma told the clerk at the cash register. "It would be helpful if you gave me the sale prices now, before the sale."

The woman stared at Helma. "Come back on Tuesday," she said.

"My trip begins on Wednesday," Helma told her. "I *am* buying all my gear from your store."

"Sorry," the woman told her.

On her return trip to the Bayside Arms, her car trunk and back seat laden high with the full-priced necessities for a back-to-nature, elemental experience, Helma drove to Ruth's house, a converted carriage house off an alley in the older, more stately section of Bellehaven, called "the Slope." She'd assembled a list of items for Ruth to bring so they wouldn't duplicate equipment they could more easily share.

Ruth's tiny lawn on the alley was overgrown and dried to brown. A few bronze chrysanthemums valiantly struggled beside Ruth's doorstep.

Helma knocked but there was no answer so she tucked the list in Ruth's mailbox, which was stuffed with flyers, ads, and bills.

Helma was just reaching for the door handle of her car when a man on a bicycle rode up the alley toward her, a bag of groceries in the wire basket on his handlebars, a bouquet of grocery-store carnations and ferns emerging over the brown top.

He stopped behind Helma's car and lowered his kickstand. It was Bradshaw, mural painter, supposed pursuer of Ruth. Painted lines of dolphins and Orca whales swam the frame of his red bicycle from the handlebars to the mud guard.

"Hi!" he greeted Helma, bright white teeth shining as he smiled, tugging on the brim of his baseball cap. A reddish brown ponytail emerged from the spacer at the back of his cap. Bradshaw was round-faced, pug-nosed, and large-eared, with tilted eyebrows and freckles. Leprechaunish, Ruth had called him.

"Hello," Helma said. "Are you looking for Ruth?"

"No," he said, glancing over at Ruth's house. "I was just going to leave her something."

He stood beside his bicycle, toying with the handlebars and waiting while Helma started her car and pulled away. When Helma reached the end of Ruth's alley, she glanced in her rearview mirror in time to see Bradshaw pull the bouquet of flowers from the grocery bag in his bicycle basket and dash down the sidewalk to Ruth's door.

It was the Tuesday before the Big Day. Helma sat at her desk in the library workroom making last-minute preparations, her new blue notebook open to the second clean page. Spread in front of her was her own modified United States Geological Survey map of the mountain region where Jekyll Glacier was located, a Northwest almanac, and the *Washington Atlas and Gazetteer*.

George Melville leaned into her cubicle. "So what's the route for the big wilderness trek?"

"We'll drive to the Hyde Point trailhead at 3600 feet," Helma said, pointing to her map, "hike to Hyde Point where we'll meet two other hikers, and from there head toward Jekyll Glacier, but only as far as Sky High Overlook." Her finger followed the line marking the trail. It looked simple enough from here.

"You're taking notes?" he asked, nodding to Helma's new notebook.

"Just jotting down a few statistics: sunrise and sunset, distances and elevations, geologic and historical facts."

George nodded. "Ah, what else does a librarian need for a good hike except information?" He squinted at the gazetteer. "Find any Bigfoot warnings?"

"Not on this page," Helma said, knowing George was referring to the grinning Bigfoot symbol in the mountains around the much shortened Mount St. Helen's, on page thirty-three of the otherwise staid gazetteer.

"I heard all this good weather has coaxed some real amateurs into the mountains, some of our less lofty-minded citizens. Be careful," he warned. "Oh, and did you see our boys in blue caught the restroom bombers?"

Helma nodded. "I understand they were high school students whose prank went awry."

"At least they must have been paying attention in chemistry class; that's encouraging."

"You picked a good time to get out of here," Eve told Helma, watching her draw the phases of the moon in her notebook. "Junie told me if the Moonbeam doesn't give in to the staff's demands by 8 a.m. tomorrow, they're going on strike."

"On strike," Helma repeated in shock, laying down her pencil. "What exactly are their demands?"

"That all references to 'nonprofessional' staff be dropped in favor of the term 'paraprofessional.' And the right to attend library conferences."

"That's not unreasonable," Helma said. "There's never been a strike in this library. I'm sure Ms. Moon will agree."

Eve raised her pale eyebrows. "That's not the point. The point is, they're making *demands*. You know how 'contrary energy' gets her back up."

Helma did. Ms. Moon had once returned a donation of desperately needed art books rather than meet the donor's demand of erasing his overdue library fines.

"Have fun in the mountains," Eve told her. "We hiked to Coleman last weekend. The snow's melted so far up it's like you're in untouched country."

In the adjacent cubicle, Harley Woodworth stood, flexing his long jaw and regarding Helma as if he might never see her again. "That's where the grizzlies are," he said regretfully. "Up where people hardly ever go."

"I'll remember that," Helma assured him.

Harley cleared his throat and said to Eve, "Can I speak to Helma in private for a minute?"

" 'Private' is not a legitimate word in this library's vocabulary," Eve said, "but I'll plug my ears if you want."

"Please," Harley said seriously, watching Eve point her index fingers through her curls into her ears.

"I have a present for you," Harley solemnly told Helma and with a grave face, presented her with a large brown bottle that had once held prescription medicine. The bottle jingled as Helma accepted it.

"Bear bells," he whispered. "They're a special frequency that won't sound loud to you but bears can hear them a mile away. Just jingle them when you get into bear country."

"That's very thoughtful, Harley," Helma said, shaking the bottle under Harley's proud gaze and suspecting that her hearing was as keen as a bear's. "Where did you get them?"

"I saw them advertised in the back of my *Safety First!* magazine. Just attach them to any piece of equipment by the little clips. They're guaranteed."

"I will," Helma promised. Bear bells. Guaranteed to do what?

Chief of Police Wayne Gallant phoned Helma while she was leaning her blue external-frame nylon backpack against the wall beside her door, tightly packed and ready to go. She'd checked each item against the list on her table and found it complete. True to her promise to Harley, she'd attached his bear bells to her blue tarp, then folded the tarp so the bells were as insulated—and soundless—as possible.

"I saw your friend Ruth Winthrop tonight," Wayne Gallant said. "She told me you were leaving in the morning. I called to wish you a good time."

"Thank you. Where did you see Ruth?"

The chief paused overlong before answering. "She was outside Joker's with friends."

Helma inwardly groaned. So much for Ruth's assertions that she was "Yes, definitely staying home to pack up and hit the sheets early; stop worrying."

"You're heading up to Jekyll Glacier," the chief said, professionalism edging his voice, as if he might be taking a statement. "Is that right?"

"Not onto the glacier, just within viewing range," Helma told him. "Ruth wants to take photographs from Sky High Overlook to use as a base for a series of paintings. We probably won't go any farther than that."

Wayne Gallant paused for the second time, then said, "I saw her new show at the Bread Biscuit."

"Did any of her subjects look familiar to you?" Helma asked cautiously.

He chuckled softly and said, "I'd say so. She's made a lot of city employees happy."

"But not the subjects themselves?" Helma asked.

"I doubt any of them will drop by the gallery," he said, echoing Ruth's claims. "Wish I had the time for a hike," the chief continued. "I've heard it's an exceptional year up there." His voice softened. "Helma, I'd like us to get together Saturday night when you come back, for dinner and . . . talk."

"I'd like that," she agreed, feeling her mouth curve into a smile of its own volition before she hung up.

She was prepared, fully equipped, well supplied, and well read. Mrs. Whitney in the next apartment had promised to feed Boy Cat Zukas. Helma's shades were drawn, her mail stopped for three days, ice cube trays emptied, trash taken out, laundry washed, dried, folded, and put away.

Helma glanced once more around her apartment, realigned her hotpads, then turned off her lights and went to bed.

Fifty-four miles of curving, steadily inclining and steadily deteriorating roads led the way from Bellehaven to the Hyde Point trailhead.

"So I slept in a little bit," Ruth said grumpily from the passenger seat as she pulled on heavy socks over her red tights. She wore a long khaki skirt that truly *did* look as if it came from a museum: fitted at the waist, flaring to her ankles. "I'm here, aren't I?"

"You weren't even packed," Helma said, nodding toward the lumpily loaded and worn Boy Scout backpack Ruth had thrown in the backseat.

"Well, it didn't take me *that* long," Ruth said, pulling down the visor mirror to apply her eye makeup. "We're talking minutes, not hours."

Helma had been forced to roust Ruth out of bed. She rarely visited Ruth's house; their meetings were at Helma's or on neutral ground, because Ruth lived in a home so devoid of order and routine, stepping inside was as disorienting as being dropped unbriefed into a Third World nation. "I can't be bothered cleaning closets and scrubbing floors," Ruth liked to say. "I'm searching for a higher order."

Helma's backpack was tucked in the trunk next to her new hiking boots which she'd broken in through twice-daily walks and by wearing them in her apartment. A new cap with a little more brim lay on the backseat and one of her three identical maps sat folded on the seat beside her.

Helma's map was based on a USGS map she'd enlarged and modified with additional color-coded details gleaned from the gazetteer and other trail guides, then duplicated and laminated at the public library.

''Have you heard a weather report?'' Ruth asked, dabbing black at her eyes.

''Clear and sunny,'' Helma told her. Not a cloud threatened the western horizon, only bright blue above them, unmarked by cirrus or cumulus. Neutral, monochromatic, and, Helma had to admit, not all that interesting once the novelty of clear skies wore off. ''Another beautiful day in paradise,'' the weatherman on Channel 5 had promised with a slightly forced smile.

''See,'' Ruth said, pointing to the sparse traffic ten miles outside Bellehaven. ''Since it's midweek, everybody's at work. When we come down on Friday, everybody will be heading *toward* the mountains. Pretty clever planning on my part, eh?''

''Very,'' Helma agreed.

Before the road began to rise in earnest into the mountains, they passed orchards bright with ripening apples, overmature and dying gardens, fields of tassled corn. The shoulders rippled with wheat-colored grasses and the dreaded invader that sucked up wetlands and forced out native plants: purple loosestrife.

In front of them loomed the green rounded foothills, slashed here and there by clearcuts that marched irregardless up and down the slopes as if a ruler and razor had been taken to the land. Brown patches in the midst of dense fir and pine. Beyond the foothills, the mountains rose blue and white, misty through the haze that had settled in the valleys from temperature inversion.

''Did you talk to your friends yesterday?'' Helma asked Ruth.

''Which ones?''

''Bill and Ariel, the hiking experts who are meeting us at Hyde Point.''

''Oh, them,'' Ruth said, gazing out the window at two horses wearing coats. ''Yeah. I talked to them. Not to worry.''

"So they'll meet us at Hyde Point at four o'clock?"

"That was the plan."

"If you want to study the map," Helma said, pointing to the folded, laminated map on the seat beside her, "I've highlighted our route with a transparent yellow marker."

"Nah," Ruth said, shaking her head. "I trust you."

Hyde Point was six miles from the trailhead, with an elevation gain of 2,500 feet. After hiking six miles up to the point, the hiker had a choice of three more trails which spoked off from Hyde Point: one heading down to the east, one heading southwest toward the bomber site on Enfield Glacier, and the third trail leading north toward Jekyll Glacier and ultimately all the way to Canada—their trail. Although Helma and Ruth would only hike as far as Sky High Overlook, Bill and Ariel planned to continue onward—properly armed with axes, crampons, and ropes—to climb on the icy fields of Jekyll Glacier.

They drove past the last few scattered cabins and into the national forest, greeted immediately by a wooden cutout of Smokey the Bear holding a shovel.

"Look at that," Ruth said, pointing to the colorful meter mounted beside Smokey. "Fire danger is extreme today. Does that mean I have to eat my hot dogs raw?"

"Only open fires are banned," Helma said. "We'll use the camp stove."

"Camp stove?" Ruth squawked, turning toward Helma. "Was I supposed to bring a camp stove? I grabbed a pack of matches."

"I brought a Primus camp stove. You were supposed to bring extra fuel. Didn't you read the list I left in your mailbox?"

Ruth looked at Helma incredulously. "That was dumb. If you wanted me to read it, why'd you leave it in my mailbox? I hardly ever look in there. Jeff the mailman sorts out my mail for me. He leaves the boring stuff in my mailbox and tucks the good stuff under my door.''

''Then that means you didn't bring a hat or gloves or a flashlight, to name a few items?''

''This is a little three-day hike in beautiful summerlike weather, Helma, not an arctic expedition. Lots of people are up here wandering around with bulging packs. I'll just borrow whatever I need.''

''Then did you bring the Ten Essentials?''

Ruth raised her chin and regarded Helma from the side of her eyes. ''I seriously doubt it but since I'm trapped in this car with you, go ahead and tell me what they are.''

''Extra clothing,'' Helma recited from memory. ''Extra food, a first-aid kit, sunglasses, pocket knife, firestarter, matches, flashlight, map, compass.''

''Well, if I don't have them, you do,'' Ruth said, pulling a rubberband from her skirt pocket and banding her hair in a rough tail. ''Did you bring a radio?'' she asked Helma.

''No. That was on your list. I knew you had a Walkman.''

''Damn.'' Ruth leaned over and turned on Helma's car radio. ''We'd better listen while we can, then.''

Rock music filled the car and Helma rolled down her window, allowing as much of it as possible to escape. When the news came on, they listened to the top stories: the vitamin pyramid scheme perpetrators had fled the state, someone had escaped from a Bellehaven halfway house, the man in the bear costume who advertised Gruffy's Restaurant by dancing on the corner by the mall had taken to exhibiting himself to passing cars.

''Exhibitionists, runaway vitamin salesmen, and halfway house escapees,'' Ruth said, flicking off the radio. She waved a hand toward the dense trees and overhanging mountains. ''Up here, that garbage sounds like crimes from the bowels of hell. Just let's not pick up any hitchhikers or talk to strangers, okay?"

Higher and higher the road climbed and twisted as they rose out of the trees and along the mountainside, the view opening up to cliffs and summits still above them, Helma's Buick straining on steep switchbacks that narrowed to a single lane. Narrow waterfalls tumbled out of black rocks and disappeared beneath the road that clung to the mountain. Here, shrubbery was turning red and gold, and on the shady side of the mountain, rocks shone brilliant green, softened with a fur of moss.

"Look at that, would you?" Ruth said, leaning forward and pointing to the snowy range across the valley beneath them that was so deep Helma couldn't see its floor. They'd risen above the valley's haze where now the blue shadows dissolved to green and finally to bare gray rock above the tree line and beneath the glaciated peaks and white summits. In the distance, green-tinged ice in a cleft marked a glacier imperceptibly moving down the mountain, too far away to decipher more than general shape and color, friendlier and smoother appearing than Helma guessed it was.

"That's north, isn't it?" Ruth asked.

Helma checked the compass mounted on her dashboard and confirmed it was. "Jekyll Glacier's over there, and Canada is only two miles beyond the glacier."

"You mean these mountains don't end at the border? They aren't all *ours*?" Ruth asked, grinning, commenting on how American interest *did* stop at the border, news and views of Canada rarely crossing into the United States, despite the country being only a twenty-minute drive from Bellehaven.

"There's a twenty-foot swath cut through the mountains along the forty-ninth parallel to delineate the border, but that's all," Helma explained.

"I wonder if they've thought of landmining it."

"There's not even a fence. We are friendly nations."

" 'Children of a common mother,' " Ruth intoned, saluting to the north. "God Bless America."

The road changed to dusty gravel and turned away from the spectacular views for a last strenuous, motor-straining climb before it entered a rough parking area holding a half dozen dusty vehicles, five of them four-wheel drives. Ruth patted the dashboard of Helma's Buick as Helma parked between a jeep and a Toyota Fourrunner. "Good car," she said as if she were praising a loyal dog. "Made it up here with the big boys."

They stepped out of the car into sunny silence. Not a single sound of civilization. No traffic or airplanes, no human voices. A pine siskin perched on a nearby branch called a high-pitched *seeee*, while the treetops huffed gentle breaths, and a ground squirrel scampered down a log to eye them curiously.

The trunk lock clicked as Helma opened it and Ruth put her finger to her lips. "Shh," she warned.

Helma froze, glancing to either side, seeing only the parking lot and cars. "Why?"

Ruth shrugged, smoothing her hiking skirt. "I don't know," she said, wincing at the sound of her own voice. "I feel like an intruder."

Helma knew exactly what Ruth meant. Even with the alien cars parked around them, she was conscious of the remoteness of this place, the sense of treading where humans were few—and insignificant. The sunny air felt thin, the colors overbright. A dark hawk soared above them, circled once and disappeared beyond the treetops.

They changed into their hiking boots and hoisted their packs to their shoulders, adjusting straps and fit, which Helma had already done, practicing between the rooms of her apartment. Every compartment and pocket was closed, her down sleeping bag tightly rolled and attached to the top of her pack.

A purple sweater poked from beneath the flap of Ruth's pack, a bulge shaped like a whiskey bottle strained against the canvas. Ruth shifted her shoulders, struggling first in one direction, then the other.

"I can help you rearrange your pack," Helma offered.

"Why?" Ruth demanded. "What's wrong with it?"

"Is it uncomfortable?" Helma asked judiciously. "Sometimes it's easier if your heavy items are packed low near the hips, especially for a woman. Your load to body weight ratio should be approximately one to thirty. So a 120-pound person shouldn't carry more than forty pounds." Helma's pack weighed 38.5 pounds.

"My pack is perfectly comfortable," Ruth said. "fits me like a glove." She twisted, shoving the aluminum frame against her hips, grimacing. "The paperboy loaned it to me, but he's a foot shorter."

Helma had walked around the Sports Corral a half-hour in her pack before she decided to buy it, then had rush ordered an inch-shorter frame.

"Well, let's hit the trail and get these bodies working," Ruth said as Helma tested the door handles of her Buick. "Kiss semicivilization goodbye for three days." Ruth turned in the parking lot and faced the distant blue valleys, kissing both hands and throwing them into the air.

The trail began beneath gigantic firs, a deep, shaded rut that immediately ascended upward, passing a wooden box on a post that held the registration book. Ruth walked past it. "Wait," Helma said. "We have to sign in."

"What for?" Ruth protested. "We're not leaving the trail. Sign in, sign out. It's like elementary school."

The last person to register had been a Judith Poole, three hours earlier; her destination, Hyde Point, where the trails branched off. Every other name was hours earlier. Helma looked up at the sun that stood high in the sky. They were beginning late and she doubted any more hikers would be climbing up the trail after them today.

Helma signed her and Ruth's names, that they'd be gone for three days, and listed their destination as Hyde Point and Sky High Overlook. While she noted their time of departure in military time in her own blue notebook, Ruth studied the registration book and groaned.

"What's wrong?" Helma asked.

"Look here," she said, jabbing a finger at the book. "My bicycle buddy, Bradshaw the muralist, is up here. He followed me, the little rat."

Bradshaw's childish scrawl held a smiley face in the upper loop of the capital B. His destination was listed as Hyde Point and "Bomber," accompanied by a tiny and accomplished drawing of a Lockheed PV-1 dropping an oversized bomb. "He couldn't have followed you, Ruth," Helma pointed out. "He signed in yesterday."

"Then he's hiding behind some stump. Just you wait." Ruth began stomping up the trail, grumbling, "Pop out grinning like a damn jack-in-the-box."

The trail switchbacked through waist-high ferns and dense trees of prehistoric proportions, growing less rutted the farther they hiked from the trailhead.

Helma led the way, falling easily into the pace she'd practiced in the park, counting "one-thousand-and-one," her heels touching ground on each "one," ignoring Ruth's, "Do you have a metronome in your head? What's that sound?" Ruth asked. "I keep hearing bells."

"Bear bells," Helma told her. "They were a gift. They're supposed to warn bears we're traveling in their neighborhood."

"You mean like a dinner bell?" Ruth asked.

The path turned hollow-sounding, as if the roots of the giant fir trees held up the earth. The trail was shaded, the sun blocked by treetops and terrain, the cooler air spicy with vegetation and moss.

"Slow down, would you?" Ruth complained. "You don't appreciate how hard it is to walk in a skirt. And don't say you told me so."

"I guess I don't need to," Helma said over her shoulder.

Ruth grunted and reached behind her for the half-empty water bottle in the side pocket of her pack, reciting as she had three times already: "During the day drink lots of water. After supper you hadn't oughter."

Turning a corner around an uprooted cedar tree, they entered a patch of blueberry bushes, thick with the dusky blue fruit. Silvery snags stood ghostly among the dark trees, pale green mosses wafted from branches like swatches of hair.

"Are you sure those are edible?" Ruth asked as Helma stripped three fat berries from a bush and popped the sweet fruit in her mouth.

"They're blueberries, Ruth," Helma told her. "Check the field guide in the lower left pocket of my pack if you have any doubts."

"A field guide? You aren't hauling enough on your back you brought *books*?"

"A few necessary volumes," Helma said, picking another handful of berries.

"If I get sick from these things I hope you're carrying a first-aid book," Ruth said, reaching for a berry. "It's funny we haven't run into anybody, isn't it?"

"We had a late start," Helma said, glancing around her at the lengthening shadows. "Every other hiker is probably far up the trail."

"Well, don't look at me like that. I'm not running a marathon, just trying to get into shape."

They crossed a dry creek bed, the depression filled with water-polished stones, and finally met two other hikers heading down in that joyful way of those who've had enough of "up." Young men laden with packs, wearing headsets and moving to a beat loud enough to be heard as they passed Helma and Ruth, waving in beat, too.

"Can we stop?" Ruth asked for the third time from behind Helma, her breath coming in gasps, her long skirt audibly swishing against her legs.

"Exhale completely," Helma advised her. "That'll remove carbon dioxide and give you more room to inhale and cause less fatigue." To demonstrate, Helma blew out her breath in a rush of air through lips shaped in an O.

"I don't need to breathe," Ruth gasped. "I need to rest." Her hair had come undone from its ponytail and stuck damply to her cheek. Her face was flushed and shiny, her eye makeup sliding down her eye sockets.

"There's a meadow called Slant Meadow about a half-mile ahead," Helma told her. "Can you hold out that long? If we stop too many times, we'll be late meeting your friends at Hyde Point."

"About Bill and Ariel . . ." Ruth began.

"If we keep going, we'll only be a few minutes late," Helma said, glancing at her watch.

"But . . ."

"The meadow's only a little farther," she assured Ruth.

Ruth puffed along behind Helma and just as they emerged from the trees into a sloping meadow of blooming purple lupines, Indian paintbrush, and heather, Ruth exclaimed, "Stop this forced march this second. I'm not going one inch farther up this trail, not a single damn inch. I'm going to sit beneath that tree. Leave me to die if you want."

"It would be better if we sat here on the trail instead of under the tree—to protect the fragile meadow flora,"

Helma told her, pointing to the trail that slanted upward across the meadow. Beneath them, the meadow seemed to slope away into the trees and down forever.

"Whatever," Ruth said, dropping her pack in the middle of the trail and collapsing to the ground, her face pink, her shirt damp with sweat. "I only care about applying bum to dirt. Ouch! Where did all these damn bugs come from? Give me twenty minutes."

"But . . ."

"They're not coming anyway," Ruth said, swatting at a black fly tasting the sweat inside her elbow.

"Who's not coming?" Helma asked.

"Bill and Ariel. Bill tripped at his line dancing class two nights ago and broke his big toe. They can't make it."

Helma dropped to the trail beside Ruth, brushing away a buzzing deer fly. "Why didn't you tell me?"

"Because you wouldn't have come," Ruth said, raising her chin defensively.

"You didn't give me the opportunity to choose."

"Well, would you have? You thought we needed a man to lead the way. There are plenty of men up here . . . somewhere. If we get stuck, we'll find one, okay?"

Before Helma could answer, wild sounds came from the pines above them at the upper edge of the meadow. Something moving through the forest, knocking into tree trunks, crashing and falling through brushes, descending toward them, fast.

"Oh God, your damn bells worked," Ruth said, struggling to her feet, "It's a bear." Helma was thinking the same thing exactly, remembering Harley Woodworth's gloomy predictions.

What was the safest course of action in a bear attack? She tried to recall what she'd read: play dead if it's a grizzly, fight if it's a black bear. Or was it the other way around?

Ruth grabbed her backpack and madly rifled through it. ''A knife. I brought a knife. We'll kill it.''

''No,'' Helma ordered. ''Drop to the ground and curl up. Cover the back of your neck with your hands to protect your spine.''

But they both stood rooted to the trail, watching the dark trees where the din came from. The tops of bushes whipped back and forth. The crashing increased, grew closer, and a shape broke from the trees, stumbling, moving too fast to keep its balance, then falling and rolling down the sloping meadow toward them.

It wasn't a black bear or a grizzly bear; it was a man and he was covered with blood.

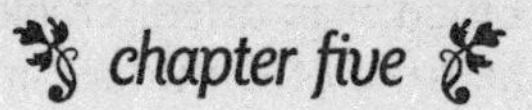

FIRST AID

For a split second after he tumbled from the woods like a rag doll and crashed just as lifelessly at their feet, Ruth and Helma stared at the bloody hiker. Ruth's hand was frozen in her backpack, while Helma's mind still foraged through wild bear evasion tactics.

Helma moved first, dropping to her knees beside the sprawled body.

"Hello," she said in a firm voice, "my name is Helma Zukas. I want to help you. Can you hear me?"

There was no answer so Helma immediately invoked the ABC procedure of life support, checking his airway, his breathing, the carotid pulse at the base of his neck.

"Cut it out," Ruth told her irritably. "I told you he'd jump out of the bushes like a jack-in-the-box, didn't I?"

"What's wrong with you?" Helma demanded, fearing Ruth was so exhausted she'd become demented. "This man is injured. He's bleeding."

"It's a trick, can't you see that? It's Bradshaw pulling some kind of a joke on us." She leaned over the prone man. "We're onto you, Bradshaw. Get the hell up."

Helma sat back on her heels, looking at the bloody man. The reddish hair and pug nose were signature. His features were obscured by blood but yes, it was definitely Bradshaw.

''This isn't fake blood, Ruth,'' Helma said. But she noticed that the blood was dried, cracking where it was thickest, across the front of Bradshaw's cotton t-shirt and along his arms. It didn't seem to come from a single source but more as if blood had been smeared on the small man.

He groaned and opened his eyes, wrinkling his forehead and staring into Helma's face as if she were an apparition. ''Do you have any water?'' he asked, struggling to sit up.

''I've got it,'' Ruth said, reaching for the water bottle in her backpack while Helma helped Bradshaw sit up on the soft grasses. He gazed around the meadow in confusion, blinking, then looked at Ruth, his eyes widening. ''Ruth,'' he said, breathing her name on a grateful breath as if all his prayers had been answered.

When she offered Bradshaw the water, he extended his hand, then caught sight of his bloody reaching fingers and froze, the water forgotten. ''Oh God,'' he said, his voice breaking. ''He's dead.''

''Drink this first,'' Helma said, taking the water from Ruth and holding the tin cup to Bradshaw's lips while he greedily sucked it down.

Finished, he took a deep breath and Helma said, ''Now tell us: who's dead?''

''Scotty,'' Bradshaw said, his face stricken. ''I found him near the trail higher up, injured. I couldn't get him to stop; he was so determined to get off the mountain, like a mad man. So, I tried to help him straight down, crossing the switchbacks on the trail.''

''Where is he?'' Helma asked, giving the cup back to Ruth.

''Who's Scotty?'' Ruth asked. ''Are you saying somebody's *really* dead up here?''

Bradshaw covered his face with his hands, shaking his head. "He's a guy I've biked with a few times. I couldn't get the whole story; he was in pretty bad shape when I found him." He looked up at Helma and Ruth. "From what he said, I figured out he and a friend named Henry, probably Henry Lanyon, were on their way to the bomber site when something happened, some kind of an accident."

"They fell?" Helma asked, remembering the harrowing tales she'd heard of the trail to the bomber.

"I don't know," Bradshaw told her. "He couldn't tell me what happened to Henry, except he was 'bumped.' " He pulled his shirt away from his body and looked at his arms in horror, as if this were the first time he'd actually been aware of all the blood. His lips trembled; he seemed unable to blink.

Helma put her arm around Bradshaw's shoulders. "Where is Scotty now?" she gently asked him.

"Back there." He pointed into the trees he'd tumbled from. "When I realized he was . . . I called for help but I didn't know where we were, so I left him to find a marker—or somebody. I thought it would be faster."

"How far back there?" Ruth asked.

"I'll show you," he said, rising unsteadily to his feet.

Helma removed the first-aid kit from her pack to carry with her, just in case. Then she and Ruth stashed their packs behind a tree and followed Bradshaw into the trees.

It was easy to spot Bradshaw's tracks; the pine-needle floor was marked by long scars as if he'd let himself drop down the hillside, using his stride to keep from falling head first.

"Just up there," Bradshaw told them, pausing, reluctant to go any farther. "By that rotting fir."

Helma led the way, slowly approaching the prone figure.

Scotty was young, in his early twenties, sandy

haired. Sun slanted down near his body in hazy shafts of light. He lay on his back, his arms at his side, blood thick on his clothing. His hiking boots and clothes were stained and dirty, as if he'd been crawling and falling for a considerable time before Bradshaw found him. Beside him lay a pack, only one.

"Is that yours?" Helma asked Bradshaw, nodding toward the orange backpack.

"Yeah," Bradshaw whispered. "I don't know where his is."

"Is he really dead?" Ruth whispered, too, her voice still too loud in the quiet trees, the body before them out of place in this beautiful spot.

Helma knelt beside Scotty's body and felt his cool neck, her heart sorrowful; he was so young. She looked up at Ruth and nodded.

"God, now what do we do?" Ruth asked. "We haven't seen anybody but you, and two hikers going *down* the mountain a while ago."

"Like I said, I called for help," Bradshaw said, reaching into a side pocket of his backpack and pulling out a black cellular phone, "but I wasn't sure of the location. Do you know exactly where we are? They're sending a helicopter."

"According to my map," Helma told him, "the meadow beneath us is called Slant Meadow."

"You don't own a car and you carry a cellular phone?" Ruth asked.

Bradshaw swallowed and took a deep breath, touching his chest and then jerking his hand away from his bloody shirt as if it were hot. "I always carry it when I hike alone. I got the idea from Scotty," he said, catching himself in the midst of a nod toward the body. "He probably had one in his pack. Maybe he already called for help. He and Henry are, were, both experienced hikers." His voice rose in despair. "I should have called as soon as I found him but he was like a crazy person, determined to get down the mountain.''

''You did what made the most sense at the time,'' Helma told him from beside Scotty's body where she still knelt. She touched the front of the dead man's shirt, noticing a hole in the fabric low and to the left beneath his ribs. Gently, she unbuttoned the stiff cloth.

''Helma, what are you doing?'' Ruth asked.

Behind them, Bradshaw took a few steps away and punched in a number on his cellular phone.

''I'm looking,'' Helma said, unbuttoning another button.

''Well, cut it out. That's sick.''

She gently separated the front of the young man's shirt. Helma was no expert but she'd had an occasion to study a forensic pathology book shelved in the closed stacks at the Bellehaven Public Library. And from that experience, she'd have to say that the wound beneath the dead man's rib cage looked very much like a bullet hole.

Bradshaw stayed with Scotty's body while Ruth and Helma returned to Slant Meadow to wait for the helicopter.

Across the meadow, the treed ridges folded one into another as far as Helma could see, until another ridge of peaks rose up behind them, snow cradled in distant clefts. No sign of civilization anywhere. Humanity might as well have disappeared from the earth.

''What do you mean, a hole in his body?'' Ruth asked as they stood side by side on the trail, peering at ranges of peaks as far as they could see, civilization and helicopters seemingly light years away, the scene too primeval for flying machines to have been invented yet. ''A bullet hole? How do you know it was a bullet hole?''

''I didn't say for sure it was a bullet hole. I said the

wound *appears* to be a bullet hole. It's definitely a puncture wound."

"He was *shot*?" Ruth went on, her voice rising, ignoring Helma's disclaimer. "How could that be? We're in the *mountains*, for pity's sake. Do you think his hiking partner was shot, too? What was his name, Herbert? Harold?"

"Henry Lanyon," Helma provided, wondering if Henry Lanyon lay dead somewhere on the mountain at that very moment, or if perhaps he had been the one who'd mortally wounded Scotty.

In the warm sunshine, Ruth rubbed her arms as if the temperature had suddenly plummeted to freezing. "There's a maniac loose up here, Helm, a frigging maniac with a gun and what have we got for protection?" She gazed at their packs, which they'd dragged from behind the tree back into the meadow. "Swiss army knives."

"You're jumping to conclusions," Helma told her firmly, raising her hand to her eyebrows and gazing into the quiet blue sky. "For one thing, I've never seen a gunshot wound up close. He may have fallen from a precipice and landed on a pointed branch that punctured his body. Maybe he fell on his knife or a tent peg. Henry Lanyon could have been hurt on their way to the bomber site and Scotty was frantically on his way for help. We just don't know."

Ruth sat down and leaned against her pack. "I hate being ignorant. I really and truly hate it."

They heard the helicopter long before they spotted it, its wump wump wump echoing through the valleys and between the peaks, sounding not like one helicopter but a squadron carrying out a surprise attack.

"Just play a little Wagner and we'll be all set," Ruth said, turning and staring in every direction as the motor grew deafening without coming into sight.

Suddenly, like an apparition, a small navy helicopter rose from behind the ridge of trees, the helmeted and goggled pilot visible through the canopy. The clearing was too steep to land, so the machine hovered at its edge while two people in uniforms jumped out, carrying a litter. Around them the meadow plants flattened and tree branches flapped in the blades' backwash. Ruth and Helma waved, then stood back from the rushing air, their hair whipping around their faces.

"Did you call for rescue?" a helmeted young woman asked them.

"Where's the body?" the man asked. He was powerfully built, tall, cool-eyed like a policeman tending to business. He carried a camera.

"Up in those trees," Helma pointed. "We'll show you."

"I don't think I want to go up there again," Ruth said to Helma. "You go ahead. I'll guard the helicopter."

Bradshaw met them halfway, the lost look on his face slipping into relief as the rescuers greeted him and took over. Now was the time for official procedures, a prescribed routine that blunted the horror. Helma stood beside a fir tree, breaking a branchlet of flat needles and inhaling their fragrance, thinking of all the rituals that accompanied death, a ritual for every occasion, from gentle death to accidental death—to murder.

When the woman rescuer shook out a black body bag, Helma returned to Slant Meadow and sat on the trail, her arms wrapped around her knees. Ruth was inside the navy helicopter, seated beside the pilot and wearing a helmet.

Within minutes, the two rescuers and Bradshaw emerged from the trees, Scotty's body in a black plastic bag. Ruth climbed down from the helicopter and they watched the litter being loaded through the side bay. The helicopter was prepared to depart. Bradshaw moved back beside Helma and Ruth, watching. The man jumped back out of the whining helicopter and approached them. "Search and rescue will head for the bomber site to look for the other hiker," he shouted. "One of you come with us to explain what happened."

Bradshaw looked at Ruth with longing. He'd changed to a clean shirt and scrubbed most of the blood from his arms. "I found him," he told the man.

"Okay, come on," the uniformed man said, grabbing Bradshaw's arm.

"Excuse me," Helma said. "Was he shot?"

The man looked away. "We can't tell anything out here," he said, and Helma guessed she was correct.

"What about us?" Ruth asked.

He stopped and looked Helma and Ruth over, then shouted over the noise of the helicopter. "I wouldn't try to hike out tonight; it's too late. There's a good place to camp about a half-mile ahead." He paused. "Do you want to go back with us?"

"No," Helma said. "We'll continue on."

"Then keep your eyes open for the deceased's pack or belongings, would you?" He paused. "Or blood. Let the sheriff know if you find anything."

Bradshaw turned once at the helicopter bay and looked at Ruth imploringly as he was pulled aboard but she waved, urging him onward and smiling.

As the helicopter rose and veered into the sky, disappearing over the next ridge, Helma realized that Bradshaw had taken his cellular phone with him. They couldn't inform the sheriff if they found any of Scotty's belongings. Neither, Helma realized with a guilty tug for even considering such a thing at a time like this, could she call the library to discover if the staff's grievances had been settled.

Ruth turned to Helma, "Why'd you say no to a helicopter ride? We could get out of here, leave the mountains to the maniacs.''

''Because search and rescue probably won't reach the bomber site on Enfield Glacier to search for Henry Lanyon until tomorrow,'' Helma told her. ''But we can search the area between here and Hyde Point before then. What if Henry's lying injured along the trail? Even though the weather's been warm, nights are cold up here. We're the only people in the vicinity who know about this accident.''

''If that's what it was,'' Ruth muttered.

''Besides, we're already here and I'm not convinced about the maniacs.'' Helma hoisted her pack to her shoulders; it grew easier each time she did it. ''And all this gear cost me a fortune.''

Ruth narrowed her eyes. ''Forget your civic conscience,'' Ruth said. ''You're just plain curious about what happened to Scotty and where his missing partner is.''

''Yes, I am,'' Helma admitted.

Ruth gazed around the silent meadow and then into the sky. ''That was surreal, wasn't it? How far's that clearing?''

''A half-mile,'' Helma said, studying her map. ''We have time to go slower and search along the trail before it gets dark. Bradshaw said he brought Scotty straight down the mountains so if Henry was able to get out under his own power, he may have stayed on the trail. The clearing's about a mile before Hyde Point. We'll hike it at first light, searching as we go.''

''But we're not going to try for the bomber site, are we?'' Ruth asked.

Helma shook her head. ''No, but since we've come this far, and if we don't find any trace of Henry Lanyon by the time we reach Hyde Point, we may as well hike to Sky High Overlook so you can take your photos.''

"How far's a half-mile?" Ruth asked.

"Normally two thousand strides equal a mile but because we're taking smaller steps, and since we'll be searching along the trail, and allowing for elevation increase and our packs, I'd say about . . . two thousand steps." Helma refolded the map.

"I guess it's too late now to have a good time," Ruth said morosely, glancing into the blue sky where the helicopter had disappeared.

chapter six

SLEEPING OUT

They hiked slowly, probing along the edges of the trail among the sword ferns and sparse grasses, searching for anything that might have belonged to Scotty or Henry Lanyon, and finding nothing, not even litter. Also, not seeing another hiker. The forest felt deserted, silent, and Ruth shrieked when a bird suddenly cried out, "Kak kak kak."

"It's only a pileated woodpecker," Helma told her, pointing to the big red-headed bird clinging to the shadowy side of a fir tree. "They're common to these forests."

Ruth narrowed her eyes at Helma. "Don't tell me you have a bird identification book with you, too?"

"All right, I won't," Helma said, toeing a piece of rotted bark beside the path that for a moment had looked like the sole of a shoe.

"Where is everybody?" Ruth asked, turning in a circle, glancing up into the treetops where a breeze whispered through the needles. "All the back-to-naturers? We haven't seen a living soul since the helicopter."

"They're ahead of us," Helma said reasonably, "because we started late."

"Will you stop nagging me about that?" Ruth moved ahead of Helma and picked up the pace. "Scotty and his buddy didn't come this way, anyway. We're not going to find a damn thing. And I'm not sure I want to, either. What if there's somebody up here robbing hikers? Maybe Scotty got drilled because he wouldn't cooperate. We could be next."

"Robbing hikers wouldn't be a very lucrative pastime," Helma told her.

"Then maybe it's a thief with low expectations."

Despite the absence of other hikers on the trail, when they reached the clearing where they planned to spend the night, it was already occupied. A faded yellow one-person tent nestled like a fat worm beneath the boughs of a spruce tree. The sun had slipped over the next mountain ridge and a cheery fire blazed in a rock ring in front of the yellow tent.

Bradshaw had said Scotty and Henry were experienced hikers and the equipment Helma was looking at was certainly well used: the faded and patched tent, a battered coffee pot balanced over the fire. Could this be the missing Henry's campsite?

"Coffee," Ruth said with longing, sniffing the air.

"Join me," a throaty voice invited and instead of a young man, a woman with short gray hair emerged from the trees, dressed in jeans and flannel. She was small, wiry, with a youthful body and the lined face of a woman approaching sixty. "Coffee's on and if you're looking for a spot to pitch your tent, I'd be happy to share my fire with you."

"Great," Ruth agreed, already shrugging off her backpack. "My shoulders are screaming uncle."

"There's a ban on open fires due to the dry weather," Helma reminded the woman as she gazed longingly at the dancing and crackling little campfire. "The fire danger's extremely high."

"It's a worry this time of year, isn't it?" she said. Her voice was husky, a "whiskey voice," Helma's father would have called it. "My name's Judith Poole."

Helma introduced herself and Ruth and briefly told Judith Poole about the dead hiker and his missing partner, although she refrained from revealing her suspicions of how Scotty had died. "Have you seen anything unusual along the trail?" Helma finished. "Signs that someone might have fallen? Or discarded gear?"

Judith Poole stood transfixed, her hands folded together at her waist, her sharp features unreadable. Her gaze was fixed on Helma but she could tell the older woman didn't really see her at all.

"Are you all right?" Ruth asked her.

"Missing," the woman whispered, still staring at nothing. "Another one."

"I beg your pardon?" Helma asked.

Judith Poole gave a small shake of her head and smiled, her eyes now sharp and intense. "Woolgathering," she said. "I haven't seen anything unusual. You two are the first to come by in either direction in hours."

"Are you up here alone?" Ruth asked. "All by yourself?"

"I prefer it this way."

Over the older woman's head, Ruth raised her eyebrows at Helma, shrugging her shoulders in a barely perceptible movement.

The first thing Helma noticed after Judith Poole's husky voice was how seldom she blinked. She watched everything with an air of expectancy, eyes intent on every motion, her gaze snapping from hands to lips, her head turning and tipping to catch every sound, either from Ruth and Helma or from the woods surrounding them. A frown intermittently appeared on her forehead, not a frown of disappointment or disapproval, but of concentration, as if watchfulness were her natural state.

"Go ahead about your business," Judith Poole told Helma and Ruth. "I'll expect you to ask me if you need help." And she sat on a log by the fire, her hands folded and back straight, eyes now turned toward the darkening forest.

Ruth's tent was as regimentally Boy Scout-ish as her backpack: a simple green triangle with zippered flaps and wooden pegs.

"I can't believe you forgot your tent," Ruth said after she'd wrestled her own into sagging order and stood beside it watching Helma spread her sleeping bag on top of a groundcloth and foam pad.

"I enjoy sleeping beneath the open sky," Helma explained.

"Since when? You haven't slept outside since you were a kid. What if it rains?"

"I brought a tarp to construct a shelter if I need to."

Ruth stood with pursed lips, her forehead wrinkled as Helma lined her sleeping bag with a modified pale green sheet and blew up her inflatable pillow, finally asking, "This wouldn't have anything to do with that time your cousin Ricky set your tent on fire, would it?"

"Of course not." Helma squeezed a line of insect repellent on the ground around her sleeping bag, admitting to herself there would be a definite comfort in opening her eyes in the middle of the night to the black vastness of a starry sky, not the enclosing cloth walls of a tent.

"I heard the helicopter," Judith Poole said as they sat around her fire. Soft darkness surrounded them, carrying a chill that was easily repelled by the fire and an extra layer of clothing. They'd eaten: Helma a pleasant bowl of reconstituted chicken soup from her store of labeled plastic bags of meals, a roll, and dried banana chips; Ruth a crushed bag of potato chips, cheese sticks, two

Reese's peanut butter cups, and, Helma suspected, a generous splash of whiskey in her coffee.

Helma had also showered, heating water on Judith's fire and rigging up her plastic bag shower from a tree limb deeper in the forest. She was beginning to think that hiking and camping might possibly be as manageable as all those books claimed.

When Ruth explained the tragedy of Scotty and the unknown fate of his partner, Henry, Judith Poole listened without comment, then gave one brief nod. "I've seen it happen before." She frowned into the fire, her gray hair glowing silver, then shoving an errant coal back into the flames with a stick, she said in her husky low voice, "My boyfriend's up here."

"Hiking?" Helma asked politely. Her boyfriend? "Are you meeting him?"

"No," Judith answered calmly, setting the stick aside and picking up her cup, holding it in both hands. "I'm looking for him."

"He's lost, too?" Ruth asked, leaning toward the older woman, her eyes wide. "Did you notify the authorities?"

Judith Poole nodded. "Over forty years ago. He was lost in an avalanche in 1954. I've come up here every year since, trying to find him."

Ruth and Helma exchanged glances, listening to the older woman's voice go flat as she repeated the tale she must have repeated many times over many other campfires.

"He was twenty-two when it happened, crossing a snow field on Jekyll Glacier during the Fourth of July holiday. I stayed home because it was my little sister's birthday. Oh my, but it was a hot one. That year the mountains had a tremendous snowpack and it was a cool spring." She sipped her coffee, still staring into the flames. "Avalanches are most frequent in the winter, but these mountains were ripe. The survivors said the avalanche crashed down from the side walls along the glacier: so quick nobody had time to get out of its way. Roger and his closest friend were lost, just lost. Gone. Three others escaped.''

She looked from Ruth to Helma, her voice turning urgent. ''You're supposed to make swimming motions in an avalanche. Remember that. Try to keep your head up. They say you can feel the air being pushed ahead of an avalanche as it sweeps toward you. The pressure changes. Your ears pop.''

Judith sighed and continued, her throaty voice turning slightly sing-song. ''It was a slab avalanche; they're the worst, you know, sheets of snow break away and thunder down the mountain, gathering more and more snow, burying whole towns sometimes, tumbling and rolling, covering everything. People are buried.'' She paused, sitting stone still. ''Now, climbers wear beacons, so rescuers can find them. If you're buried under the snow, you can hear people searching for you, calling your name, begging you to answer. But if you call back, they can't hear you; you're just using up your air. So a beacon would be a comfort while you waited, don't you think?''

Helma shuddered at the thought and they sat silently for a few minutes, the only sound the crackling of the fire.

''But,'' Ruth said, ''after almost fifty years, what's left of . . . I mean, what can you hope to find?''

Judith turned her frown on Ruth, her sharp eyes snapping. ''Why, Roger, of course. Snow moves. He's buried on the glacier somewhere. Glaciers flow. Roger will eventually flow out of the mountains with the rivers of snow and into the Nitcum River. From there, he'll travel to the sea. It'll happen long after I'm dead, in the next century. Don't you think that's an undignified and lonely end?'' she asked Helma and Ruth, and then continued without waiting for their response. "If I don't find poor Roger first, who will? Years from now, he'd only be a curiosity. He *expects* me to find him."

Helma and Ruth stared at this healthy, perfectly reasonable-appearing woman explaining how bodies were preserved by snow and cold, her alert eyes touched by light, her voice as matter-of-fact as if she were discussing preserving peaches. "Sometimes they can even detect the last meal, hundreds of years later," she finished.

Helma's tea was cold, Ruth's cup was empty. Judith Poole jerked once as if she'd thumped to earth, and said, with a cheery little chortle, "Oh my, I sound daft, don't I? Except for going down the mountain to buy provisions, I've been up here six weeks. I couldn't let such good weather go to waste."

The night was clear, the sky a wonder. While Ruth and Judith slept behind the flaps of their tents, Helma lay awake, her flashlight and unsheathed Swiss army knife beside her head, watching the thick stars through the mosquito netting attached to her hat.

A waxing moon hung in the southwestern sky, Venus beneath it. Long ago, Helma and her cousin Ruby had concocted a poem to recognize the phases of the moon:

If the light is on the right,
The moon will grow in might.

If the light is on the left,
The moon will soon be-reft.

To which her cousin Ricky had added:

If the moon is big and round,
Watch out for the werewolf hound.

Now and then, rustling sounded from the trees on the edge of the clearing and once she caught the trill of distant howling, but as long as she was able to see the outlines of tents and trees against the sky, none of it was threatening or even disturbing and she finally drifted off into a deep sleep where Scotty the dead hiker and his friend Henry marched down the mountain trail together, happily singing ''Home on the Range'' in perfect harmony.

Judith Poole was gone. In the misty morning light, even the stones from her campfire ring had disappeared. No sign of her banned fire remained.

''She was weird anyway,'' Ruth said as she stirred instant coffee into cold water, watching Helma do stretching exercises recommended in *Hiking Without Pain*. ''Isn't hiking all day with a thousand pounds on your back enough?'' Ruth asked. ''You have to *exercise*?''

''We're walking, not stretching,'' Helma explained. ''Stretching limbers up your body. Try it; you'll be less tired.''

''I'm not tired at all,'' Ruth said, then continued, ''in fact, maybe Judith Poole was never here at all, did you think of that? All that talk of her dead boyfriend melting down the mountain—we might have experienced a 'Twilight Zone' moment, under the influence of the great outdoors.''

''I don't think so, Ruth,'' Helma said, dropping one raised arm and pointing to the holes in the ground from Judith's tent pegs. ''She was just exceedingly quiet leaving.''

''Spooky,'' Ruth commented. ''Maybe she's the halfway house escapee we heard about on the radio.''

''She was too familiar with all her camping gear,'' Helma said. Still, Helma *was* surprised that Judith Poole had managed to pack up and leave the clearing without disturbing Helma's slumber.

"I didn't hear helicopters this morning," Ruth said as Helma helped her adjust her pack straps. "Did you?"

Helma shook her head. "Maybe the search team is coming up on foot."

"Or maybe Henry wandered out on his own."

The higher they hiked, the sharper the air grew, clearer, so radiant that their shadows felt weighted. The light from the sun was brighter, more stark and painful to the eyes, and Helma gave in to wearing the sunglasses she'd reluctantly bought for the trip.

The view opened up as they grew closer to the tree-line: trees gave way to rocks and open alpine meadows, range after range of purple mountains' majesty in morning light, the impossible rise and fall of bottomless valleys and jagged snowy peaks.

And the higher their elevation, the more groundwater they encountered: seeping from rocks and trickling downward from melting snowfields. Moss and lichen, mountain heather still in bloom, bellflower and lupine just opening as if Helma and Ruth were traveling backward through time, from early autumn to summer to spring.

As they approached Hyde Point without finding any sign of Scotty or Henry's passage, Helma began to suspect Ruth was right: neither man had passed this way, at least not in an emergency state.

Behind her, Helma heard the sound of flesh slapping flesh. "These damn bugs keep going up my skirt. I think they're carrying portable drills."

Helma walked with her hands beneath her shoulder straps, lessening the pull of her pack. "I have insect spray," she offered, "although it doesn't impress them much."

"No thanks. It clashes with my perfume."

Finally, the trail rose onto the knobby rocky promontory of Hyde Point, bare of trees, with ridges leading off in three directions, three different trails.

"Top of the world," Ruth breathed. "It would be a sacrilege to try to take pictures of this."

Beneath them was the evidence of old slides, pines tipped and growing in huddles as if they'd picked up their roots and slid down the sides of the earthy cliffs together.

"Glaciers." Helma pointed out the higher, deeper reaches of the mountains where crevasses glowed aqua green.

A white cloud, smooth as a domed cap, hung above Mount Baker, while the rest of the sky remained autumn blue.

"I think I'm in heaven," Ruth said. "At least I'd think so if my body wasn't screaming it was in hell. Criminal we've never been here, isn't it?" Ruth asked. "Right in our backyard." She slapped at the inside of her elbow where a deer fly had settled. "So we made it this far without finding a sign of Henry Lanyon. What do we do now? Are we absolved of further responsibility? Free to go on to Sky High Overlook in the name of art?"

Helma spread her map on a boulder warmed from the sun, orienting map to terrain. "We have three choices, four actually, if you include the trail we just climbed. That trail leads to the bomber," she said, pointing to the southwest, where a dim trail clung to the rocky slopes, turning and twisting through scree.

"No way, Helma Zukas," Ruth said, shaking her head. "Let the big boys do it."

"We don't have the proper equipment anyway," Helma told her regretfully, knowing that without the appropriate gear or expertise, the route to the bomber would be a foolhardy choice.

"Search and rescue could have come up that way,"

she said, nodding to the east below Hyde Point, where their second choice, a well-worn trail, led down the opposite side of the range. "They're probably at the bomber site by now."

"I wish we had a radio so we'd know," Ruth said, then held up her hand. "Don't say it."

A whistle sounded beneath them and a marmot stood on his hind legs on a rocky outcropping, warning of their presence. The groundhoglike rodent's fur rippled. He was fat and glossy, preparing for winter.

"That's the Pitted Range," Helma said, pointing to the blue mountains to the north. "Canada's only a few miles away."

"So this is our third choice and the way to Sky High Overlook?" Ruth asked, taking a step along the narrower trail that curved to the north along the ridge top.

They strode to the top of the world in the brilliant sunshine, leaving behind the tragedy of Scotty and Henry, accompanied every step of the way by deer flies that bumped and bit until they got what they wanted or died trying. Every plant and rock was distinct, sharp, as startling as new vision. Then the trail dipped from the ridge into twisted and wind-shaped trees.

They met three elderly women, short and sturdy and as similar as sisters, each carrying a walking stick and wearing a fabric sun hat.

"Gorgeous view ahead," one of the women said as they passed. "Worth every step of the way."

"You remind me of a photo I have of my mother," another woman said to Ruth. "Climbing the mountains in a khaki skirt."

And the women were gone, disappearing around the next bend.

Two hours later they reached Sky High Overlook, interrupting two raucous crows squabbling over a fragment of fish, so far from water. The overlook was a high cliff, jutting over the valley like the stony prow of a ship. Gnarled and stunted trees grew back from the cliff amid leathery bushes and stubborn grasses.

"Let's eat here," Ruth said, unbuckling her waistband. "Then I'll draw out my Brownie. But first . . ." She made motions into the bushes.

Helma took in the view, staying well back from the edge, raising her eyes and noting how a second cloud had joined the first over Mount Baker, both of them now puffed like cauliflower. Behind her, a hint of haze seemed to be gathering in the trees, barely perceptible and if Helma looked at it for too long, she couldn't see it. It was just as well they were heading back down the mountain as soon as Ruth snapped her photographs.

Helma breathed deeply. Growing up in the flatlands of Michigan she'd imagined mountains to be as remote as foreign countries, accessible only on rare and expensive vacations.

"Hey, Helm."

It was the tone of Ruth's voice that spun Helma around so abruptly she scraped her leg against a rock.

"Look at this, would you? I found it lying on its side in those bushes."

It was an orange backpack, one of the serious, expensive kind Helma had seen on "National Geographic" specials. Well used, a patch on one pocket, faded and stained. A sierra cup hung from the frame by a leather lace.

"A hiker might have stashed it there while he took a side trip," Helma suggested.

"It didn't feel stashed; it felt *dropped*, do you know what I mean?"

Helma knelt and searched through the flap pockets until she found a notebook, and then a smudged and well-folded map.

"What do you think?" Ruth asked.

Helma opened the notebook. On the flyleaf it said, ''Scotty Irvine.'' ''It's the hiker's pack,'' she told Ruth.

''*Our* hiker?'' Ruth asked, dropping beside Helma. ''Our *dead* hiker? I thought they went to the bomber site. That's in the opposite direction. How'd his pack get here?''

''I don't know.'' Helma opened Scotty's map and began to read the notebook, touching her finger to points along the map.

Ruth stood and peered over the edge of the overlook. ''Do you think they could have fallen here? Nobody could live through *this*.''

''Do you remember exactly what Bradshaw told us Scotty had said?'' she asked Ruth.

''Something about the bomber,'' Ruth said, still gazing over the ledge. ''And about Henry being bumped. Why?''

''According to this notebook, they were climbing on Jekyll Glacier.''

She rose and hunkered down beside Helma, tucking her skirt around her legs. ''Where does it say that?''

''Look, here's yesterday's date and here's an entry for 9 a.m.: Tower Ford, and here it is on the map.'' Helma went back and forth, matching map to notebook.

''Then why did he say something about the bomber?''

''They didn't fall here at Sky High Overlook,'' Helma said with certainty.

''Maybe they were on their way back down the mountain.''

''No. See this entry: False Bridge. That's on Jekyll Glacier.'' She looked at Ruth. ''It's his final entry.''

Ruth bit her lip. ''So you think they had an accident—or Scotty was shot—at False Bridge?''

''I'd say *something* happened there.'' Helma refolded the map and put both it and the notebook in her own pack. ''False Bridge was Scotty's last entry.''

"Because he was already injured and *couldn't* record anything else," Ruth suggested. "Check his pack. Bradshaw said Scotty usually carried a cellular phone."

Helma searched through all of Scotty's possessions, spilling them onto the rocky ground, but there was no phone.

She stood and removed the silver whistle that hung around her neck, then stepped away from Ruth, took a deep breath, and blew the whistle three times, each blast lingering in her ears like a scream.

Ruth raised her hands to her ears, then demanded, "What in hell are you doing?"

"Signaling for help," Helma told her. "Three whistle blasts is the universal signal for help, three of anything."

"Three gunshots, too?" Ruth asked.

Helma nodded, counted to thirty, and blew three more times. She took the whistle from her lips and waited for a response: a shout, another whistle, a concerned ranger emerging from the trees.

But there was only silence.

"We can't wait. Let's go," she told Ruth, hastily repacking Scotty's backpack, all but his sleeping bag, which she attached above her own. "We may need this," she said. They hauled Scotty's pack into the trees where Ruth had found it and left it there.

"Back to Hyde Point?" Ruth asked. "To go for help?"

"We're closer to Jekyll Glacier," Helma told her. "Henry may be there, injured, while the searchers are looking for him at the bomber site on Enfield Glacier. We're going to Jekyll Glacier."

chapter seven

CROSSING OVER

Like a scene in a movie, they heard it before they reached it: the steady roar of falling water. A lot of water.

Except for occasional stands of stunted trees, the trail climbed above timberline, growing narrower and rougher, curving along the mountainside among tumbles of rock, brilliant green lichen, and plants that grew madly during their short lives. The path traveled close enough to snow that they stepped across muddy mires of trickling water and smelled the frigid breezes that blew across ice.

Jekyll Glacier lay ahead of them, visible when the trail turned, "flowing" for miles from a deep cleft on the north face, a gigantic, green-tinged, surprisingly dirty river of undulating ice and snow, as craggy and broken as a mountain itself.

"That must be Tower Ford," Helma told Ruth, raising her voice as she paused to listen to the thundering water. "It's on the map. Scotty and Henry crossed it."

"I hope there's a bridge," Ruth shouted back to her.

There wasn't. The water crashed down from the snowfield above them, racing and spraying over boulders as big as automobiles. No gently babbling stream here, only white movement creating its own miniature climate and winds. Spray hung in the air, moistened their faces, clung to their hair. They stood beside the fifteen-foot-wide raging torrent, uneasily studying it. Around the stream, the fragile high-country grasses and plants glowed spring green; the flowers were as luminous as tropical blooms.

Above them, wispy clouds stretched across the sky in long feathers and when she'd last glimpsed Mount Baker, Helma couldn't see the summit, only gray-bellied cumulus clouds rising around it like smoke as if its quiescent volcano had come to life. The weather report they'd listened to on the car radio had gaily promised sunshine, only sunshine.

There were two improbable spots to cross Tower Ford, one a series of water-slicked rocks that were spaced a foot or two apart and looked as stable as bowling balls, and the other a narrow wet log angled at the foot of a ten-foot-high Niagara Falls. Every few seconds water splashed up over the log.

"I guess this is it, right?" Ruth asked, shouting close to Helma's ear to be heard. "We might as well turn back and look for some hunk with a cellular phone. Call in the cavalry, or the mounties."

Helma agreed. She'd rather ride an elevator than cross this tumultuous waterway by either available method. "Let's leave our packs here and walk up the stream so we can see the glacier."

Fifty feet higher along the rushing water and the view spread before them to the width and depth of Jekyll Glacier, white and ragged, monstrous. They chose a rock large enough for both of them to sit on its still-warm surface and view the glacier. Ruth pulled a bag of peanuts from her pocket and held them out to Helma.

"Doesn't it seem to be getting cloudy to you?" she asked.

"A little, but in an average year, the mountains are cloud-free only one day out of six."

"Not a little cloudy, a lot cloudy. Look, you can see those streaky clouds filling up the whole sky. It's colder, too."

"It only seems that way in the shade," Helma assured her, noting how the clouds cast blue shadows across the glacier's snowfields.

"The bugs from hell are gone," Ruth said, chewing a mouthful of peanuts. "Have you noticed *that*? If *bugs* flee, you can bet something nasty is in the air. I mean, bugs are equipped to survive nuclear annihilation."

Helma removed her binoculars from their case, wiped the eye pieces with a camera cloth, and scanned Jekyll Glacier. The frozen river poured down a chute between mountains, miles long, not actually dirty but as the glacier melted, the rocks it held were exposed, giving the glacier the appearance of having rolled through mud. Crevasses glowed green, dropping out of sight, and along the edges of the glacier, the ice was ridged into jagged pillars taller than buildings. At the glacier's lowest periphery, its snout lay tattered and pathetic, melting into the scoured earth.

Jekyll Glacier was desolate, magnificent, an arctic wasteland. Helma carefully swept her binoculars over its surface, seeing no movement, no sign of anything alive. The sun suddenly broke through the accumulating clouds and Ruth jabbed her in the elbow, knocking the binoculars away from her eyes. "What's that?"

"Where?" Helma asked, lowering her binoculars.

"Something flashed. It's gone now, but it was right over there."

Helma aimed the binoculars where Ruth pointed. At first she saw only thick glacier ice but then, instead of a flash, she glimpsed color out of place on the ice: green. She turned the focus, trying to bring the object closer.

The shape moved, then stopped, then moved again. "I think it's a person," Helma told Ruth. "No, it's definitely a person wearing green. Look, he's fallen."

"Henry Lanyon," Ruth said, standing up on the boulder.

"He's traveling the wrong way," Helma told her. "Deeper into the mountains."

Ruth took the binoculars and said, "Do that whistle thing again."

Helma, with all her might, blew her whistle. Three shrill blasts that took all her breath. The sounds were lost in the crashing water, the vastness surrounding them.

"He didn't even turn around," Ruth said, gazing through the binoculars. "There's no way he could hear that puny sound."

Helma peered up at the lowering sky, now nearly solid with clouds, then at the obviously disoriented green figure stumbling over the treacherous glacier, and finally at the crashing stream in front of them.

Ruth sighed and shook her head in resignation. "Nobody's going to pop out of the mountains to save him, I guess. This is where our Girl Scout genes kick in."

"I was never a Girl Scout," Helma told her, feeling her heart beat in heavy thuds.

"Obviously." Ruth tipped her head, studying Helma. "Scared?" she asked.

"Just thinking," Helma said. "The log over the stream looked safer than the rocks." She rose from the boulder and they returned to their packs, again surveying their two choices of passage.

"I will if you will," Ruth said.

"You go first."

"Why me?"

Helma hesitated. "Because you're braver than I am."

"Only in situations where brains are not a requirement."

Helma removed a length of nylon rope from her pack and tied one end around a rock and gave the other end to Ruth, tugging the rope taut.

"Here we go," Ruth said and casually stepped onto the log, bouncing as if she were testing its strength as the water frothed up toward her, splashing her boots.

"Do you want to hold my hand?" Helma shouted to her from land where she held the rope loosely, ready to jerk it if Ruth slipped.

"No. I'm okay."

And Ruth simply strolled across the log over the wild water through a mist of droplets to the other side of the stream, not hesitating, not slipping on the wet log, her skirt billowing around her as she stepped onto dry land. It took her less than five seconds.

On the opposite side of the cascading stream, she stood on a square rock and waved to Helma. "Come on! Nothing to it." Ruth tied her end of the rope to a rock and Helma detached hers and gripped it firmly in her right hand as she prepared to step onto the log.

Ten minutes later and Helma had inched her way to the middle of the log, scooching across on her bottom, her pack bumping against her back and water frothing beneath her like the devil's cauldron. All she could hear was water; her face and legs were drenched. The water swirled and roared and pounded beneath her in endless movement. She couldn't go any farther. Her muscles simply refused to obey her desperate mental commands. She sat where she was, clutching the rope with one wet and red hand and the log's crumbly bark with the other, staring into the torrent, helplessly thinking of sinkholes, collapsing bridges, and falling elevators, knowing without a doubt that she was doomed.

Suddenly a hand roughly gripped her shoulder and

Ruth's voice screamed into her ear. "Move your butt before this damn stick breaks under the two of us!"

Ruth tugged and Helma resumed inching across the log, her eyes closed, her movements guided by Ruth's painful grip, until Ruth finally said, "Okay. You're on land."

For a few minutes Helma sat on a rock beside the stream, wiggling the blood back into her fingers and feet and refilling her lungs. She wiped her face on the red t-shirt lying across her lap; it was one of Ruth's. When she was able to form words again, she said, "Thank you," to Ruth, who stood on the rise above her, holding Helma's binoculars to her eyes. Helma hadn't even felt Ruth remove the binoculars from around her neck.

"You owe me," Ruth said. She leaned forward as if that would bring the view through the binoculars closer. "He fell," she said. "And this time, he didn't get up."

Helma rose, walking unsteadily for the first few steps, stumbling once on a rock, and joined Ruth. Henry Lanyon, if that's who it was, was now a still green slash on the glacier's back. He was farther away but lower than they were, which would make the trip to his side a little easier. Ruth pointed slightly above them, toward the moraine, the edge of the glacier.

"See there?" Ruth asked. "That dirtier streak in the ice above the rocks? It looks like an on ramp to the glacier. Kind of a trail, like other hikers have used it."

There did appear to be a trail through the tumble of wet rocks and ice pinnacles and onto the body of the glacier. From this distance, the crevasses were clearly visible, but would they be so simple to see as they traversed the glacier? In the other direction, the trail they stood on continued downward, beneath and around Jekyll Glacier's snout and according to the maps, continuing to Canada.

Ruth lowered the binoculars and announced, "The

sun's disappeared, in case you hadn't noticed.''

Helma had been well aware of the changing conditions. Behind them, a foggy mist had topped the slope and was gradually advancing, hot on their trail. Mount Baker had vanished behind clouds heavy with gray undersides. *Mountain weather is unpredictable,* the hiking books had advised, *disconnected from weather at lower elevations.*

''We'd better hurry,'' Helma told Ruth, glancing down at the folded map. No more streams between their position and the hiker, only something the wounded Scotty had ominously named ''False Bridge.''

They'd taken a dozen hurried steps, Tower Ford's splashing fading behind them, when a thunderous groan sounded across the mountainside as if the mountain itself were shifting in pain.

Ruth froze, staring up at the flanks of snow above them. ''Is that an avalanche?''

''I think it's the glacier,'' Helma told her. She'd read about the creaks and moans of glaciers as they made infinitesimal adjustments in their massive flows.

''Doing what?''

''Breathing.''

''As long as it doesn't sneeze.''

They gradually drew nearer to the glacier, which was far more distant than it appeared, following the faint trail across the scoured and rocky landscape as barren as the moon, slipping on scree. They didn't have the right equipment: no ice axes or crampons and nothing on the desolate landscape to use for improvisation. Helma knew this was foolhardy, dangerous. But not that far away a man lay in the snow, surely in danger for his life.

''Oh, God,'' Ruth said from behind Helma. ''And here I am in a *skirt*. What price vanity?''

Again Helma removed her rope from her pack, tying one end around her own waist with a bowline knot and the other end around Ruth's, leaving twenty feet of slack between them.

"Is this necessary?" Ruth asked.

"Prudent," Helma assured her.

A raindrop landed on Helma's cheek as they climbed the trail in the rock-laden and crystalline snow leading onto the glacier. A thick stillness had descended, not silence, but nonmovement, as if the two women traveled across a still-life.

Leading the way, Helma kicked each foot into the steep wall of snow, testing the depression before she put her full weight into the step, climbing upward toward the broad surface of the glacier.

"I'm pooped already," Ruth said, her breaths heaving.

"Rest between each step," Helma told her. "Let your leg go lax while the other one pulls you forward."

"Like patting your head and rubbing your stomach at the same time," Ruth said.

"It's called a rest-step."

"Yeah, yeah. Don't tell me; you learned it from a book. Can't we leave our packs here and pick them up on the way back?"

"Better not," Helma advised. "We may need them."

Even in the cloudy light, Helma squinted through her sunglasses and pulled her hat brim lower as they entered the white landscape. The rain had increased, but the drops were fine, hardly more than mist. The path across the glacier's pitted snow was faint but they stayed on it, trusting it to be the safest route.

"When we're above the hiker," Helma explained, "we'll travel down the glacier to him."

"My legs are freezing," Ruth said.

"There are two stocking caps in the lower compartment of my pack," Helma told her, stopping so Ruth could get to them. "Put one on."

"I said my legs are freezing, not my head."

"A hat will help. You lose 30 percent of your body heat through your head."

"Are you sure it's not 29 percent?" Ruth asked.

"My information said 30 percent," Helma told her.

"God forbid I argue with the printed word," Ruth said, pulling the stocking cap on with both hands.

They heard it again: the rushing of water. Helma glanced around them, but all she saw was snow and ice in every direction.

"It's under us," Ruth whispered, grimacing and pointing down at their feet.

"False Bridge," Helma said, listening.

The snow felt solid but from beneath them came the crash and splash of water as wild and tumultuous as Tower Ford, only invisible, directly below their feet. But how far beneath?

"Avoid any rocks," Helma warned Ruth. "In all the sun we've had, a rock warms up and melts the snow beneath it. If you step on it, the snow collapses."

"Swell."

They crossed the snow gingerly, on mental tiptoe, the rope stretched taut, breaths held, arms out like tightrope walkers, feeling as if they walked on cartoon air that might suddenly drop them like stones.

On the other side of False Bridge, they stopped and layered on more clothes against the dropping temperatures and frigid breezes. Now the sky was not only sunless but seemed to be growing darker.

"Look," Ruth cried when False Bridge was finally only a whisper behind them. "He's moving again."

The green figure appeared to be crawling at right angles from the direction they'd originally watched him travel.

"He's disoriented," Helma said. "He's circling."

They left the faint trail and headed toward the hiker,

keeping the rope's length stretched between them, traveling downward along the glacier's length, half sliding, landing heels first in the snow.

"Help!" Ruth yelped and Helma threw herself forward, tightening the rope before she turned around to see what had happened.

Ruth floundered, one foot in a narrow fissure to her thigh, her skirt billowing out. Helma remained where she was, her feet planted, until Ruth pulled her leg free, fluently cursing the world in general and Washington state in particular.

Moisture dampened Helma's face and she squinted across the glacier against the backdrop of mountains, making out an approaching mist, descending toward them like a wall.

Her nose was cold. The temperature had definitely dropped; it hadn't been so noticeable during the strenuous upward portion of their hike. She increased her speed, her eyes sharp on the descending vista in front of her, alert for cracks and fissures, heading for the green shape that once again lay still in the icy snow. Her pack bounced painfully against her back and her shoulders felt rubbed raw. Cold perspiration clung to her torso.

Like dream walking, it seemed to take forever to reach the collapsed hiker, until finally they dropped into the snow beside him. He lay curled on his side like a child, one arm extended at an impossible angle, his face blotched and patchy inside the hood of his jacket.

"Henry?" Helma asked. "Are you Henry Lanyon?"

The man's eyes fluttered as if he were struggling to open them, then he went lax, exhaling a deep and contented sigh. Beneath his green flannel shirt he wore a second heavy shirt, the cuffs pulled down over his hands. His wool pants and hiking boots were wet. He was older than Scotty, perhaps in his early thirties, with a two-day growth of beard.

"We can't drag him *up* this glacier," Ruth said as she rubbed the man's bare hands between her own, nodding toward the route they'd just descended, which now looked impossibly steep.

Helma was already busy. She opened her pack and pulled out her blue tarp, unfolding it and spreading it beside the injured man, the bear bells Harley had given her, and which Helma had attached to the tarp, jangling loudly. Then she unfolded her map and showed it to Ruth, allowing herself a moment's congratulations for having the foresight to laminate it, watching the misty rain bead on its surface.

"See how these trails twist through the mountains?" Helma told her. "To the east beneath us, the trail we were originally following crosses under the snout of the glacier. There's an emergency hiker's cabin not far from the snout, to the northwest side of the glacier. There's another one to the west but it's too far away. These cabins may be very primitive but we'll be protected from the weather until help comes." If the cabin still existed, Helma thought. The map she'd copied the emergency cabin symbol from had been seven years old.

"If we can move him that far," Ruth said. Henry Lanyon moaned and Ruth added, "That's a heck of a goose egg on his forehead. And I think his arm's broken, don't you?"

"It appears to be," Helma said, looking at his twisted arm, then scanning the misty glacier, now unable to see the tracks she and Ruth had made a few minutes earlier. Had Henry fallen into a crevasse and managed to free himself after Scotty went for help? But what danger had Scotty faced on the trail? Another set of tracks—unsteady and irregular—meandered near Henry's. Even in his desperate and injured state and over uneven ice, he'd doubled back on himself.

"Helm," Ruth said quietly, staring above them. "That's snow."

Not mist as Helma had believed, but a steadily advancing flurry, tiny flakes so close together they mirrored fog. They weren't going to outmaneuver the weather or outrun it. She gave Ruth her extra pair of gloves and together they slid Henry onto the tarp, trying to avoid bumping his arm, grateful he was unconscious.

"I hope somebody's putting a gold star by my name even as we speak," Ruth muttered as she gripped the wadded tarp at Henry's feet and they began working their way down the glacier.

They slid downward, falling, bracing themselves with their heels, nothing substantial to hang on to, nothing to grab.

Then, creeping up at their backs, the snow overtook them, enveloping them in white. Miniature tender flakes that softened their grunts and struggles and clung to their clothes and hair like powdered sugar.

Helma's compass hung on the same chain as her silver whistle and every ten steps she paused, wiped it off, and checked their direction, correcting their rightward descent and hoping they were aiming for the emergency cabin.

Suddenly, a sound rang out below them and Ruth screamed, tripping first, then falling and letting go of her end of the tarp. She lunged for the material but caught her boot on the hem of her skirt and stumbled into the snow while Helma tried desperately to hold on, falling backward, struggling with the slick material.

But the fabric slipped helplessly through her hands and she watched in horror as Henry Lanyon slid away on the blue tarp, gathering speed as he raced down the glacier and disappeared into the falling snow, the bear bells gaily ringing.

chapter eight

RUNAWAY MEN

Helma and Ruth sat in the snow, their mouths open, staring after the vanishing tarp that carried Henry Lanyon, hearing the tinkle of bear bells and the whisper and swish of the laden tarp skimming over snow and ice.

"Good Lord," Ruth breathed. "We lost him."

"We have to retrieve him," Helma said. "Hurry! The crevasses!"

But neither one of them moved, mesmerized by the fading descent and jingle jangle of the runaway tarp.

"Did you see how fast he took off?" Ruth asked. "I never owned a sled that went that fast."

"This isn't the time . . ." Helma began. "This is terrible. He could be killed."

"Oh God, I know it!" Ruth clapped her hands together in a sharp sliding motion. "Whoosh. Gone. Just like that."

"Ruth, this is an emerg . . ." Helma tried again, beginning sternly, seriously; what was wrong with Ruth? But their eyes met and widened. Ruth's mouth contorted and she burst into guffaws, helplessly doubling over.

Helma was horrified and mortified to discover herself

sitting on a glacier in falling snow and dropping temperatures, having just lost an injured man to an unknown fate, helplessly *giggling*. She pressed her lips closed, only to have moisture escape her nose and wet her upper lip.

It was the altitude, surely. The altitude and the dire circumstances of their situation, the accompanying stress.

Ruth covered her mouth with both her hands, tears streaming down her face, rocking, opening her mouth to speak but dissolving into paroxysms that echoed across the glacier. She and Helma bumped together, Helma's eyes filled with tears. "Whoosh!" Ruth repeated.

Helma wiped at her face, and then took herself firmly in hand, struggling to stand on the coarse snow, conjuring up the image of an unfortunate sparrow that had slammed into her window and dropped dead on her balcony, of all the truly dire things that could happen on an uncontrolled slide down a glacier, followed by various beloved and dead relatives, their caskets trailing past like boxcars, until she was appropriately and soberly composed.

She tipped her head, hearing through the muffled snow the sound that had startled them into releasing the tarp: a whistle. She quickly raised her own whistle from around her neck and blew three answering blasts.

"Hello!" a man's voice came faintly from somewhere beneath them. "Are you all right?"

"Maybe we knocked Henry into consciousness and now he's pissed," Ruth said, collapsing into giggles again.

"We're all right," Helma called, already walking heels first downward toward the voice, sharply jerking on the rope tied to Ruth's waist.

The snow had reduced visibility to fifty feet, accompanied by a wind that rose and fell on its own mysterious currents. No longer tender flecks, the snow had turned icy, the flakes sharper, whipping against Helma's face like grains of sand. When she was close enough to decipher a dark upright silhouette in the whirling snow, Helma called out, "We had an injured party with us."

"I've got him," the man replied. "I didn't expect you to let him go."

"Neither did we," Helma said. "Thank God."

"Thank *you*," Ruth added to the man.

Henry Lanyon lay snugly in the blue tarp, not even ruffled from his trip. Holding him from descending any farther was a man, stocking-capped and goggled, his reddish moustache hung with ice crystals, snow clinging to the shoulder seams of his blue and green jacket.

"We've been watching you come down the glacier for the last half-hour," he said. "I came out to help when the snow began."

"Out of where?" Helma asked.

"The emergency cabin," he shouted in a sudden gust of wind.

A second figure struggled uphill toward them. "Is it Roger?" a woman's smoky voice called between sharp intakes of breath. "Did you find Roger?"

It was Judith Poole who, apparently, had not yet located her boyfriend's body. She was hatless, her short gray hair scrambled, face pink and eyes burning on the blue tarp.

"No, I'm sorry," Helma told her. "It's an injured hiker, the partner of the man who died yesterday. His name's Henry Lanyon."

"Oh." Judith stopped, her interest waning, eyes now moving up onto the snowy glacier as if her boyfriend Roger might be trailing along behind them. Here I am; sorry to be so late.

In another sharp gust of wind, Helma pulled her collar

upright to protect her neck. "How far to the cabin?" she asked the man.

"Five minutes, maybe ten, carrying him. We'd better get started." He nodded toward Judith, turning his back toward the wind. "She says worse weather's moving in." He held out a gloved hand. "Sorry. My name's Brentley Utterson and I'm the only man at the cabin."

Beside Helma, Ruth snorted and Helma fleetingly wondered what Brentley meant.

They maneuvered down the tongue of the glacier and then through a grove of twisted pine, each of them burdened with a corner of the tarp while Lanyon lay pale and silent. Ruth and Helma offered fragmented explanations of the dead hiker and how they'd discovered his partner Henry struggling on the glacier in a state of disorientation. As if they'd already agreed between themselves, neither Ruth nor Helma mentioned the possibility of foul play in Scotty's death.

"Hypothermia," Brentley Utterson commented with authority. "Warmth and liquids will fix him right up."

Around them as they descended in elevation, the snow lessened, turning once again to gelid rain that fell at an angle, feeling colder than the snow.

"Has he said anything?" Brentley Utterson asked. With the goggles and cap, Helma couldn't clearly see his features, only that his chin was rounded and he sounded middle-aged.

"Nothing," Helma told him. They were back on solid ground, scattered with rocks and low growing tufts of sedge. She glanced over her shoulder at the falling snow on the glacier above them, wondering if this rain would turn to snow as both night and temperatures descended.

The emergency cabin, a squat log building the size of a small garage with narrow windows and a solid wooden door, nestled into a protected slope. Smoke wafted from a cement-block chimney newer than the building itself.

"Careful of that rock," Utterson warned as they lugged Lanyon to the edge of the tiny porch outside the cabin, its posts carved with initials and dates.

"BonBon!" Brentley Utterson called. "Open the door."

The door remained closed and Brentley Utterson called again, cajoled actually. "Open the door, BonBon."

Judith Poole made an impatient snort and dropped her side of the tarp, forcing Brentley to grab for it or tip Henry Lanyon onto the rocky earth.

"That girl . . ." Judith said as she pushed open the wooden door.

"That girl" was the first object to come into focus in the gloomy interior of the emergency cabin, a vision in bright pink. She posed beside a cast-iron stove, her pale hair curled and waved, one pink-encased leg gracefully bent at the knee, manicured hands covering her assuredly pink mouth, eyes round and horrified above a straight and elegant nose.

"Give us a hand, BonBon," Brentley said. "Clear off that bunk."

But BonBon only stared, rocking her shoulders. "Is that a body?" she asked in a quavering light voice. "Is he . . . dead?"

"Oh, God. A stereotype," Ruth muttered wearily. "Even her voice is pink."

"I've got it," Judith Poole said, swiping clothes and a pack off one of the lower bunks.

Five sets of iron bunks were crammed into the tiny well-worn room. A cast-iron woodstove squatted in the cabin's center next to a tipsy picnic table. A battered shelf was attached to the wall. That was all.

"He's not dead," Helma told BonBon, who emitted a high happy shriek. They gently lifted Henry onto the bunk and pulled the tarp from beneath him. He groaned.

The bruise distorted his face but Helma could see his high cheekbones and the small bump near the bridge of his straight nose, as if it had once been broken. His eyes were deep set, heavy browed.

"Does anyone here have medical experience?" Helma asked, feeling for Henry's pulse and finding it weak and slow.

"I know CPR," Brentley Utterson said. He removed his hat and unzipped his expensive green and blue Gore-Tex jacket. He was in his early forties, successful looking, dressed in new earth-tone pants and a corduroy shirt that still held store-bought creases. Brentley was slightly below average in height, soft-bodied and soft-featured—almost chubby, the type of man who had to struggle to keep extra weight at bay, eventually losing the battle. In his expression and the line of his shoulders, Helma detected an air of worldly disappointment, all perceived in a flash before Helma turned her attention to the injured man, whose bluish lips moved and then went still.

"Is there . . . blood?" BonBon asked, still keeping her distance.

"No," Brentley assured her. "At least none is visible." He pulled a rolled sleeping bag from the higher bunk and unfurled it. "Let's get him warmed up."

"According to my sources," Helma said, "the most effective way to warm a person with hypothermia is for another person to lie down next to him. He needs a gradual source of body heat to bring his own body temperature back to normal. Ideally, both should be naked."

"I'll volunteer," Ruth offered, already moving to take off her sweater.

"You're cold yourself, Ruth."

"He's kind of cute," BonBon said, leaning over the bunk and gazing at his face, unconsciously touching her own forehead at the precise spot of Henry's swelling. "Do you think he'll die?"

"Not if we properly care for him," Helma told her. "You've been inside so you're probably the warmest of us all. Lie down beside him and we'll cover you with sleeping bags and stoke up the fire."

BonBon took a step back from the bunk. "I won't do it if you're going to take off all his clothes," she said petulantly, her lower lip protruding.

"Such delicacy," Ruth muttered.

"Well, I won't," BonBon said resolutely. "Not naked. And that's that."

Helma felt Henry Lanyon's clothing. His pants were only wet around his knees. "He's wearing wool," she said, "so it should be all right. But we'll remove his shirt and boots." Lanyon was long and slender, six feet tall, Helma guessed, his damp brown hair cut by a stylist, not a barber.

"All right then," BonBon said while Helma unlaced Henry's hiking boots and Ruth gently removed his shirt.

"Be careful of his arm," Helma warned her.

"Somebody get him a hat," Ruth said. "We lose 30 percent of our body heat through our heads."

"We do?" BonBon asked.

"That's why we have hair," Ruth said with authority.

BonBon giggled once and gingerly stretched out on the narrow bunk next to the injured man while the others covered the pair with sleeping bags.

That done, they finally went through the formality of brief introductions. Helma surveyed her surroundings, just the same as she would if she'd entered a stranger's home, observing the comforts and dangers. There was only one entrance, the solid plank door BonBon had declined to open. She noted more closely the five sets of bunks with only tightly woven metal springs, how one of the windows was boarded over, shards of glass still scattered on the floor beneath it. The picnic table was wooden, carved with graffiti like the front posts of the cabin: *DL & SP 1994. Joyce loves Mike. Paul Bunyan slept here.*

A tattered poster of animal tracks hung on one log wall and on another, a reminder to notify the ranger station regarding used or missing supplies. The cabin smelled of burning firewood and beneath that, the odors of disuse and misuse. An animal had chewed the wood around the bottom of the door. In the rafters of the peaked ceiling, a silvery wasp nest hung suspended, either empty or dormant.

"How much firewood is there?" Helma asked.

"There's a rick beside the building," Brentley said, and for the first time, Helma noticed how Brentley, who still stood beside Henry Lanyon's bunk with his arms crossed, was contemplating her.

"Are you trying to take over?" he asked, smiling a smile that didn't reach his eyes. His skin was the type that burned easily and his sunglasses had left white rings around his eyes.

"Oh oh," Ruth muttered from beside Helma. "You've stepped on somebody's manly toes."

"Of course not," Helma told Brentley. *Always first attempt to appease the irritated patron,* Helma had learned in library workshops. "I'm only saying aloud what I'm sure you'd already planned."

"Spare me," Ruth commented.

Brentley continued to stare at Helma, then snapped his fingers. "The library. That's where I've seen you. You're a librarian."

"Yes I am," Helma admitted.

"That explains it then," Brentley said, smiling unnecessarily.

"I didn't know librarians hiked," BonBon said from the bunk.

"My, they look cozy," Judith said, nodding to BonBon and Henry and combing her silver hair with her fingers. ''Roger and I used to lie like that and watch the stars sometimes. It was perfectly innocent, of course,'' she finished sadly.

Henry Lanyon didn't appear cozy in Helma's eyes; he appeared wan and, yes, lifeless.

She checked the contents of the cabin's clearly marked emergency supply chest, located in a storage bin beneath the floor, while the others stayed close to the stove or hovered nervously near Henry and BonBon as if they required chaperoning. The phrase ''milling around'' entered Helma's mind.

The emergency chest was empty. According to the list inside the door, it should have contained sleeping bags, dried food, and a first-aid kit, but all that remained was a faded booklet titled, ''Pack it Out!'' stressing the value of cleanliness in the National Forest. Helma was disappointed not to find a broom and dust pan.

''Vandals,'' Judith commented, looking over Helma's shoulder. ''Anybody can get up in the mountains with all this good weather, including the riffraff. We're lucky they didn't torch this place. It isn't like it used to be.''

''There are also amenities,'' Brentley said, his voice lowering like a fervent announcer with good news. ''Just follow the rope I tied to the post beside the door.''

''Amenities?'' Ruth asked from the stove, where she stood so close, steam rose from her back. ''Oh, you mean an outhouse. Amenities, that's cute. But why a rope?'' She'd pulled off the wet stocking cap and her dark hair bushed around her head like a corona.

Brentley nodded toward Judith. ''It was Judith's idea. She predicted this weather, claims it's going to get worse.''

''You could have told us that last night,'' Ruth said to Judith.

''Last night I didn't know the weather was about to change,'' Judith said. She glanced out the window and added, half to herself, ''We can't predict everything we'd like to.''

''*I* figured it might,'' Brentley said, dusting off his hands as if he'd just completed a job well done.

''Then you three met each other here in the cabin?'' Helma asked.

''Well, no,'' Judith said. ''I ran into Brentley and BonBon on the trail and warned them.''

''She *insisted* we come with her to the cabin,'' BonBon whispered from Henry Lanyon's bunk, where she lay half across his body. ''Brentley didn't believe her.''

Brentley's nostrils actually flared. He smoothed down the front of his shirt. ''We still had time,'' he said defensively. ''We could have made it down.''

''*No*,'' Judith told him with calm certainty. ''You could't have.''

Through the narrow window beside the door, Helma saw that small hard flakes of snow, like the snow they'd encountered on the glacier, had now replaced the rain, falling in a straight trajectory from the sky. ''We'll need to bring in more wood,'' Helma said, ''and move the rest beside the door. We don't know how long we'll have to stay here.''

''I don't suppose anybody's carrying a cellular phone?'' Ruth asked hopefully. She'd deserted the stove and was testing the bunks. ''These things will be like sleeping on a bread rack,'' she said, leaning on the woven springs.

''I wouldn't think of bringing a phone, Ruth,'' Brentley Utterson said. ''I hike to get *away*. This weather will let up and we'll be able to hike out in the morning.''

''We *do* have an injured man,'' Helma reminded him. Brentley had a habit of fervently repeating a person's name, like a telephone salesperson.

"Then I'll report it to the ranger as soon as I'm off the mountain."

"You'd just bogey off and *leave* us?" Ruth asked.

"Wouldn't that make sense, Ruth, to send help?" Brentley asked. "I could probably get down the mountain fastest." He blotted his moustache with his wrist and zipped his jacket closed. "But right now I'll bring in the wood," he continued. "You girls see what you can do to make this place more comfortable."

There was no mistaking the tone of his voice, the swagger in his walk to the door. Ruth's face flashed red. Judith Poole's gray hair seemed to bristle. "Girls," she repeated softly.

"Dividing us into hunters and gatherers?" Ruth asked. "the herd and the stud?"

"Now, now, Ruth," Brentley said, turning and smiling indulgently as if he'd love to pat Ruth's head if only he could reach it. "In the wilderness the traditional values hold sway. Equality's not an issue out here."

"I see," Ruth said with dangerous sweetness. "I'd fetch your slippers if you'd been thoughtful enough to pack them."

He laughed appreciatively and went on with his manly duties, unaware of the pairs of eyes boring into his back.

"We could tear him to shreds and sprinkle the remains over the glacier," Ruth suggested.

The winds increased to shrieks, rattling the loose-fitting windows and creating drafts that swirled and chilled near the floor. Henry Lanyon's body temperature rose despite the brisk air; his face regained color and his breathing deepened, although he didn't open his eyes. BonBon left his bunk, her flushed face beaming with success.

"When I was a little girl, I wanted to be a nurse," she said as she tidied her clothes.

"Instead of what?" Ruth asked.

"Oh, I work in an office," BonBon said. "Sales. What do you do?"

"I'm an artist."

BonBon frowned at Ruth, then shaped her mouth into an O. "Oh, you're *that* Ruth Winthrop," she said, her eyebrows raising. "From your work, I didn't expect you to be so tall."

"Most people don't," Ruth told her. "My paintings look like a short person's art, don't you think?"

"Mmm," BonBon murmured, her smooth forehead creasing.

There was no mistaking the bad chemical mix between Ruth and BonBon; the air bristled between them. Helma found it curious; they had no history, they barely knew each other's names.

Helma poured a small amount of water from her water bottle into a cup and held it to Henry's lips, just letting the liquid moisten his swollen mouth.

"I'll do that," Judith Poole offered.

Helma gave over her place beside Henry to Judith and wiped off the picnic table with a dishcloth she'd packed in her lower outside backpack pocket, then went to work lining the worst of the window cracks with rolled sheets of paper towel from her pack. "Could you bring in a fairly straight pine bough with your next load?" she asked Brentley.

When he did, she fashioned it into a rough broom, and using the "Pack it Out" brochure as a dustpan she swept the area around one of the bunks before spreading her sleeping bag on the metal springs.

Brentley continued to bring in load after armload of firewood, his shoulders bending under each armful, his self-confident swagger gradually wearing away to weariness. Once Helma stepped forward to help and Ruth grabbed her arm. ''Don't you dare. This is his show. Enjoy it while you can.''

''Are you and Brentley together?'' Helma asked BonBon when Brentley had left the cabin for another load.

BonBon vigorously shook her head, her wavy hair swaying. ''I was supposed to meet friends at the trail-head but they didn't show and Brentley was just starting up the trail so I tagged along.'' She pointed to an expensive, feminine, pink backpack leaning against the wall. ''I bought new equipment and I didn't want it to go to waste.''

''I've never seen a pink backpack before,'' Ruth said.

''It's called pale lavender,'' BonBon corrected.

''It looks pink to me,'' Ruth countered.

''Well, yours looks like a regulation Boy Scout pack,'' BonBon said with exaggerated politeness. ''Are you a troop leader?''

''Hardly. This is my birthday hike.''

As soon as Ruth said it, Helma could see she was sorry. BonBon's eyes glittered. ''Which birthday?'' she asked.

''My thirty-fifth,'' Ruth told her, her chin rising.

BonBon sniffed and flashed Ruth a patronizing smile, obviously believing thirty-five was generations older than she was.

''Is this your first hiking trip?'' Helma hastily asked BonBon.

BonBon nodded. ''Since I was a little girl. But I go to the club every day. Aerobics. I'm the top stairclimber in my class.'' Unconsciously she moved her feet as if climbing invisible steps.

''And where's your class?''

''In Seattle. I don't leave Seattle very often—except in an airplane, I mean.''

''He opened his eyes,'' Judith suddenly called out.

They rushed to Henry Lanyon's side. The tip of his swollen tongue ran along his lower lip and he glanced from face to face in apparent confusion, stopping at BonBon's.

"Are you Henry Lanyon?" Helma asked.

He shifted his gaze to Helma, studying her from chin to forehead, then ear to ear and finally nodding, his lips moving without sound.

"Are you injured?" Helma questioned, biting back all her other questions: What had happened to Scotty? Why were the two of them separated? Why had Scotty said they were at the bomber site? Those questions would have to wait until later.

His lips moved again and she bent close to his mouth. "Shoulder," she understood him to say, then his eyes fluttered and closed.

"The temperature's still dropping," Brentley said when he brought in the last load of firewood. He held up the tab of his jacket zipper, which held a miniature compass and thermometer. "Thirty degrees out there," he announced. "And the rain's completely turned to snow."

Helma stood at the window, watching the thick flakes twirl and blow past the window, binding together in clumps, turning the world white unbelievably fast. She knew snow from her youthful years in Michigan and this was serious snow, the kind that could steadily fall for days, the kind of snow that fell when winter began in earnest. She doubted they'd be leaving in the morning. In fact, it might be time to assess their situation and review wilderness survival techniques.

As she continued to watch the descending flakes, a tall and bulky shape emerged from the twisted and whitening trees, making its way toward the cabin without hesitation. Helma blinked as a thick curtain of snow momentarily obscured the figure, then squinted to be sure it was real. Before she could turn and tell the others, rapping sounded so forcefully on the cabin door she wouldn't have been surprised to see the wood bow inward.

chapter nine

WELCOME TO OUR WORLD

"Oh God," Ruth said, turning and staring at the cabin door, which still seemed to resonate. "Does a Sasquatch knock?"

"Is that like an abominable snowman?" BonBon asked, raising a fluttering hand to her mouth without touching her freshly glossed lips.

"Or a yeti, as they're called in Tibet," Brentley offered from the bunk where he sat rubbing his shoulders when he thought no one was looking.

The cabin was filled with the curious white light of snow, brightness coming from everywhere and nowhere. The members of the accidental group paused, expectant, no one making a move to answer the door, all eyes shifting to Helma, who stood closest to the metal latch.

She reached for the latch as Judith Poole bit her lip and covered her heart with both her hands, staring at the door with a hopeful glint in her eyes.

A large figure in a black hooded parka stomped inside, shaking snow from its shoulders and head, shrugging off a large contoured backpack from which more snow avalanched to the floor. Because of the stranger's size, taller than Ruth and broad-shouldered, Helma concluded it was a man. His eyes were covered with amber goggles, a red wool scarf hid the lower half of his face, his parka hood was pulled over his forehead.

He stomped twice more and began removing his outer clothing while the inhabitants of the cabin watched silently, as if an alien had materialized in their midst.

He emerged: a thick head of blond, nearly white, hair, a jaw from the superhero comics Helma had seen young boys toting, shoulders that stretched against the seams of his corduroy shirt, loose twill pants that damply clung to his slender hips and muscled thighs.

BonBon ran her tongue over her lower lip. Ruth shook her hand as if she'd accidentally plunged it into hot water. A slight smile played around Judith Poole's lips and she absently smoothed her gray hair with her hand, while Brentley Utterson rose from his bunk and stretched himself as tall as he was able, squaring his shoulders and thrusting out his chest, his mouth grim.

Helma, the only person who still seemed capable of speech, cleared her throat and beckoned the newcomer toward the woodstove in the middle of the cabin. "Stand closer to the fire to warm up. I'll make you a cup of tea."

He removed his amber glasses, exposing pale blue eyes and thick blond eyelashes, but only glanced toward the stove as if it held no possible interest to him. "I'm fine, thanks," he said as he registered the presence of the inhabitants of the cabin, showing no surprise, his voice deep and without much inflection. "No problem."

Helma considered the handsome man in front of her while snow puddled and melted on the floor around his feet. His teeth were white and even, his lips sharply defined.

"I'm Helma Zukas," she said. She pointed toward the others, who introduced themselves while the stranger nodded briefly to each of them without favoring anyone with a smile or special acknowledgement. His cheeks were attractively rosy from cold. A rivulet of melting snow ran down his neck, which he ignored.

"Who's that?" he asked, motioning toward the injured man on the bunk.

"Henry Lanyon," Helma told him. "His hiking partner was killed yesterday and we found him wandering on Jekyll Glacier today, a short while ago, actually, just as the snow began."

"Lucky," he commented. "What happened to him?"

"We don't know yet. He hasn't been conscious enough to tell us."

Ruth stepped forward, her hand out graciously, her smile more brilliant than Helma had seen in weeks. "Welcome to our little bivouac," she said in a sultry voice. "Cozy and dry, good company. You wouldn't happen to have come equipped with a name, would you?"

"Whittaker," he said.

"Oooh," BonBon breathed, released from her trance and stepping up beside Ruth as if Whittaker were reeling her in. "That's a nice name, like the poet."

"What poet?" Ruth asked.

"You know, Walt."

"That's Whitman," Ruth said with unnecessary emphasis. "Walt Whitman. What we have here is Whittaker." She turned back to the blond man. "Now, is Whittaker your first name or your last name? Please don't tell me it's your entire name."

"You mean like the man who sledgehammers watermelons?" BonBon asked.

"Very good," Ruth told her.

"Newcomen," he told Ruth as he slipped his goggles

into his parka pocket. He was obviously used to female attention and appeared unfazed, his pale eyes distant. "Whittaker Newcomen."

"The newcomer's name is Newcomen," Ruth said, exactly what Helma was thinking. "Curious coincidence."

"Not much room in here," Whittaker commented, lifting his bulging pack and pointing to the unclaimed bunk in the corner, "but I'll stay out of your way and hike out as soon as the snow lets up."

"That's a big pack," Ruth commented, nodding to Whittaker's tall and tautly stretched green backpack. "Are you on an extended vacation?"

"Only a few days," he said in a tone that discouraged any more questions, turning his back on the group and lugging his gear to the corner bunk, watched by all of them except Judith Poole, who was gazing out the window at the feathery gobs of snow that drifted densely to earth until the winds caught them and tossed them in capricious directions.

"It snowed like this when I came up looking for Roger in '73," Judith Poole said. "I was lucky to make it out alive. Nonstop for seventy-two hours. I built a snow igloo, that's what saved my life." She shaped an igloo with her hands, softening its dome and rocking her body slightly as if it were a good memory. "Snow does funny things to you. You lose definition."

Brentley Utterson began to bustle with the air of a host being put upon by too many unannounced guests. He opened the woodstove and shoved two more logs into the snapping flames. "Everybody has to pull his weight around here," he said loudly and pointedly. "This situation calls for cooperation, not slinking off into a corner."

"Getting testy, aren't we?" Ruth asked, looking down at Brentley. "Feeling the stress of long confinement?"

Brentley puffed, pursing his lips, then whisking his hands together. "We'll have to share our food."

"He's right, Ruth," Helma agreed, ignoring Brentley's satisfied grunt. "That's the most sensible plan: to combine all the food and ration it, calculating three days' worth."

"Three days!" Ruth said, turning to stare out the window at the falling snow. "You're joking."

"As a precautionary measure," Helma assured her. "The snow will let up sooner than that, I'm sure."

"Don't count on it," Judith Poole warned. "Seventy-two hours. The average annual snowfall on Mount Baker is over five hundred inches, some years *much* more."

"It would be best to pool our flashlights, lanterns, and fuel, too," Helma suggested.

Brentley frowned. "I just bought a new krypton flashlight/lantern combination," he said.

"It'll be very useful," Helma said.

"But it's expensive. I don't . . ."

They were interrupted by a groan from Henry Lanyon and quickly gathered around the injured man's bunk.

"What's wrong?" BonBon asked him, bending over his bruised face and speaking close to his ear. "Do you hurt somewhere?"

"You might raise his head," Whittaker Newcomen said from his bunk, where he was removing items from his backpack.

He spoke with such calm assurance that Helma asked, "Are you a doctor?"

"Nope," he said as he set a small black transistor radio beside a ball of wool socks.

"A radio," Helma said. "Is it operational?"

"It was this morning."

"May we listen to it?"

Whittaker shrugged. "It won't change anything."

"There may be a report on whether a search party is looking for us."

He handed her the radio and Helma turned it over in her hands, noting AM and FM dials, and idly asking, "Where did you receive your medical training?"

"At the . . ." he began, then stopped, his hand inside his pack, and regarded Helma, his pale eyes cool and unreadable. "I'm *not* a doctor. Whatever problem your friend's having, I'm not trained to treat it."

"But you clearly have more experience than any of us."

He turned his broad back to Helma and she carried the radio to the wooden picnic table where she brushed off the seat before sitting down. When she clicked the black dial, she was greeted by static on the FM channels, hearing once the faint garbled sound of pulsing South American music. She switched to AM and immediately found two stations: one from Canada and one from Bellehaven, recognizing the perky theme music similar to an advertising jingle which had been written by a team of fifth-graders in a countywide competition.

"A radio!" BonBon squealed, deserting Henry Lanyon for Helma. "Are they talking about us yet?"

Ruth pulled back her sleeve and glanced at her watch. "Five minutes to news. I hope they pronounce our names right."

Whittaker Newcomen reclined on his bunk, leaning against his rolled sleeping bag. He closed his eyes but Helma noticed how much space his presence occupied in the small cabin. They were all aware of Whittaker, no matter how much he seemed to seek invisibility.

Only dark spots remained on the floor where the snow had melted into the fir planks. Helma's companions, except for Whittaker and Henry, gathered around the picnic table and the radio, their expessions avid.

An instrumental verion of a Bob Dylan song ended

and the radio announcer's tinny voice called out. "Gotchernews for ya!" They listened to a report of the city council meeting where rising garbage collection fees had been debated, then an item about the fraudulent vitamin sales fugitives who'd fled Seattle for parts unknown.

" 'Heaven's Nutrients?' " Ruth asked. "What kind of goofy name is that?"

"It was one of those pyramid schemes," Judith Poole offered. "I heard all about it."

"Vitamins and age-defiers? Who'd be crazy enough to *take* a bunch of snake oil like that, let alone buy into a pyramid scheme?" Ruth asked, shaking her head.

"People have high hopes," Judith said.

"Take Heaven's Nutrients and hope to high heaven," Ruth said. "Time will not be defied," she intoned, touching the lines at the outer edges of her eyes, "no matter how much money you spend or how many pills you take," not noticing how her cabinmates avoided each other's eyes.

"Shh," Helma said. "The announcer just mentioned the library." She bent her head closer but the news item was over. All Helma had heard were the words "Bellehaven Public Library" and "Friends." What could it mean? The library a top news story? Had the strike taken place, after all? And "Friends," he might be referring to the Friends of the Library, the very active group of volunteers who raised funds for books and equipment, but *what* about them?

"An unexpected snowstorm is pounding the Cascades," the newscaster finally said. "hampering the search for a missing hiker whose companion was killed yesterday. Police have yet to release any details of the hiker's death. Several other hikers are also still in the mountains."

The announcer went on to give the Bellehaven school

hot lunch menu: pigs-in-a-blanket, and Helma switched off the radio.

"That's it?" Ruth asked incredulously. "We're 'several other hikers'? And look at this: we've got the 'missing hiker' tucked in right here and now. Send the damn helicopters, why don't you?" she said to the radio.

"Helicopters can't fly in this weather," Helma reminded her. "Besides, it's only been a few hours since the snow began. They won't realize we're missing for a while."

"Yeah," Ruth said glumly. "Not until we come floating down the Nitcum with Judith's boyfriend, Roger."

"Oh," Judith said, covering her mouth, her eyes instantly tearing up.

"That was mean," BonBon told Ruth, putting her arms around the older woman.

"Sorry," Ruth mumbled. "Really, I apologize. Being cooped up like this is getting to me."

"We haven't even been here three hours," Helma pointed out to Ruth.

"Time is immaterial; it's the state of mind, the lack of choices, the powerlessness of it all." Ruth ran her hands through her dark hair. "I may go mad."

They combined the food from all their packs and lined it on the rough wall shelf in plain sight from every bunk, although from the generous and hearty manner with which everyone commingled their caches, Helma suspected there remained stashes of trail mix and chocolate bars tucked in various corners. She herself had kept aside a packet of M&M's, but only for prudence's sake.

"Look at this," Brentley, who was taking his turn watching over Henry Lanyon, said.

He'd uncovered Henry's stockinged feet, pointing to the way Henry's wool stockings clung to his feet. The material was damp, darkened; why hadn't they noticed?

"This doesn't look good," Brentley said. "Should I pull them off?"

BonBon's face turned white as snow; she swayed as if she might faint. Judith led the pink young woman to the table and helped her sit down.

"That's blood," Ruth said. "How did he cut up his feet?"

Whittaker rose from his bunk and towered over them, studying Henry's stockinged feet. "It looks like a bad case of blisters," he said. "He probably got his feet wet and just kept hiking. You should have got him out of those clothes first thing," he said, glancing at Helma as if she had failed in her responsibilities. In resignation, he added, "I'll take care of it. Where's a damn first-aid kit?"

"I've got one," BonBon said, and left the table to retrieve a top-notch first-aid kit from her shiny new backpack, averting her eyes from Henry's feet. The kit was larger than Helma's, still sealed with security plastic.

"Hospital in a box," Ruth commented as Whittaker broke the seal and lifted the plastic lid to expose all the sparkling, sanitized components: bottles, bandages, and emergency implements, even a snakebite kit.

"What's wrong with it?" BonBon asked defensively. "This is what the outfitter said I needed."

"Overkill, so to speak," Ruth said. "You were taken."

BonBon raised her pert nose. "Not if we're finding a use for it now."

"Good point," Ruth said amiably.

When Whittaker pulled out scissors, bandages, and ointment, as one, the group shifted to the other side of the cabin, facing away from the operation.

"It'll be dark soon," Judith commented. "And colder." She sighed, gazing through the window. "If it keeps snowing, I won't be able to search the mountains again until next year."

The falling snow now had a grayish cast as light faded from the day. Between them, they had four lanterns, five flashlights, and plenty of fuel. At least there wouldn't be a shortage of light.

Helma opened her notebook and checked the figures she'd entered at the library. "Sunset is at 7:35 tonight," she said.

Brentley bent uncomfortably close to her, peering at her notebook. "I admire librarians, Helma," he said, chuckling cozily. "You're all just chock full of facts. What else do you have in that little book of yours?"

Helma closed her notebook and leaned away from his suspiciously friendly round face. "Only private information," Helma told him, gazing at him until he stepped away, his face darkening.

Whittaker tended to Henry without fuss or comment and Helma's confidences regarding the injured man began to rise. Whittaker removed Henry's damp clothing, replacing it with his own oversized clothes.

"Here are the contents of his pockets," he said, setting a bandanna bulging with small items on the table. Ruth fished out a key chain that held a medallion and two keys: a car key and a smaller key. She jangled the keys to catch everyone's attention. "Our buddy Henry's an accountant," she said, reading the medallion attached to the key chain. "A certified public accountant. Maybe if we save his life he'll do our taxes for free."

The handkerchief also held a tightly wound roll of twine, eighty-two cents, a battered Swiss army knife, which Helma inspected, remembering the puncture wound in Scotty's body. The knife was clean. BonBon held up a pair of sunglasses broken across the bridge.

"What's this?" Judith asked, picking out a disposable syringe, its needle protected by an orange cap.

"Oh my and tsk tsk," Ruth said. "What was our Henry into?"

Whittaker silently laid a laminated business-size card in the middle of the table next to the bandanna. Helma picked it up and read aloud, "Henry Lanyon: Insulin-dependent diabetic." She looked up at Whittaker. "This was in his pocket?"

Whittaker nodded.

"I don't suppose there were any bottles of insulin in his pocket, too, were there?"

"None," he said.

"Diabetic?" BonBon repeated.

"Any bottles of insulin in your super duper first-aid kit?" Ruth asked BonBon.

"None," Whittaker repeated, answering for BonBon.

"Well, we just won't let him eat anything," Ruth said. "Then he won't need any insulin, right?"

"Unfortunately, the human body needs insulin whether we eat or not," Helma said. "After a time, often a few days—or less—without insulin, the diabetic slips into a coma." She looked at Whittaker for confirmation and he nodded. "We found Scotty yesterday . . ." Helma began.

"So they were probably separated yesterday morning," Ruth finished, "and he probably hasn't had insulin in thirty-six hours. So he's ready to free fall into a coma. What do we do?"

"He'll be thirsty," Whittaker said. "He's been physically moving the past day so that activity might have lowered his need for insulin and bought us a little time. Exercise reduces high blood sugar by getting glucose into the cells."

"If the snow doesn't stop," Helma said. "We'll have to take him down the mountain."

"And risk all *our* lives?" Brentley asked. When he saw five pairs of eyes turn to him, he amended, smoothing his red moustache. "I mean, it's probably not a good idea to move an ill man. We can do more for him by keeping him warm and safe here. The snow will stop."

"Seventy-two hours," Judith pronounced. "I remember."

Night fell completely before their reconstituted dinner was eaten and camp dishes washed in melted snow water, which Helma first heated on the stove and purified with iodine tablets despite Judith's claims that it wasn't necessary. The little cabin glowed in lantern light.

"If the circumstances were different, this could be cozy," Brentley commented, glancing around the room.

"Yeah," Ruth agreed. "Six people trapped in a snowstorm with a mortally ill person *does* put a damper on the fun quotient."

Outside, the wind whistled and bumped against the little cabin. Between gusts, Helma had the sensation that snow was silently piling itself over the cabin and when morning broke, they'd find themselves buried until spring beneath a smooth lump of white.

"Is that thunder?" BonBon asked, rising to her feet, her hands hovering at her cheeks.

They all froze, listening to the booming rumble that seemed to come from all around them.

"It's just the glacier shuddering," Judith said. "There isn't any danger."

Helma remembered a March day on Blue Lake when she was a child, playing on the ice while her father set tip-ups in ice holes, fishing. A sound like a gunshot had crashed across the sunny day, echoing back and forth between the treed shores. "It's going to break up pretty quick," her father had said, taking Helma by the hand and leading her to solid ground.

* * *

Without discussing the arrangement, they'd divided the sleeping quarters by sex: women to the left, men to the right, although each bunk was hardly an arm's length from the next. Of the five sets of bunks, the women shared theirs, each of the men occupied a lower bunk with no one above them. Brentley slept next to Henry, and Whittaker had claimed the bunk in the corner, as far as he could possibly get from everyone else in such close quarters.

After they had divided the night into two-hour shifts to watch over Henry and keep the fire going, retiring to their bunks seemed the next logical move.

Ruth's bunk was above Helma's and Helma tucked her space blanket under the edges of Ruth's metal springs so it draped around her bed. "If you're so modest," Ruth asked, "why not wait until everybody else is in bed and climb in under cover of darkness?"

"I prefer my privacy."

"Huh. Don't we all?" Ruth leaned closer and said in a low voice. "You know why there aren't any details on the news about Scotty's death, don't you? Because it *was* murder and the cops are still trying to figure out the who what where when and why. And you know what else? Our good deed might have saved the murderer's life: our boy Henry."

"Then why was Scotty trying to find help for Henry?" Helma asked in a whisper, their voices concealed beneath a conservation BonBon and Judith were holding regarding the merits of golden retrievers versus Labradors.

"I don't know. He was delusional?"

Behind her space blanket curtain, Helma washed herself as best she could from a pan of water and prepared to slip inside her sleeping bag, wearing a t-shirt, flannel pants, and socks. Her backpack leaned against the end of her bunk, much lighter now that her food and her books had been removed. She brushed her teeth with a dry toothbrush and put a single roller in the stubborn wave on the left side of her head.

That completed, she climbed into her sleeping bag, scooching downward into the liner sheet with the zipper done up, certain that no matter what the circumstances, after the physically and mentally demanding day behind her, she was going to sleep well.

But she'd barely begun scooching when her feet bumped against something hard and cold resting at the bottom of her liner sheet. Surprised, Helma froze, holding her breath. When the object didn't move, she cautiously reached down inside her bag and grabbed the object.

Before she pulled it into the murky light of the cabin, she knew what she held. Someone had slipped a pistol inside her sleeping bag.

chapter ten

NIGHT WATCH

In her bunk, behind her silvery space blanket curtain, surrounded by the near darkness, Helma gingerly backed out of her sleeping bag and sat up, laying the pistol on her lap. It gathered into itself all the dim light of her small space and reflected it back, but even its reflection was dark, not shiny as from a mirror's glassy finish but like the still surface of a black pool at the bottom of a deep black hole.

A gun in her sleeping bag. Helma bit her lip and stared at the weapon, her hands folded close to her waist. There certainly hadn't been a gun in her sleeping bag the night before when she and Ruth had shared the meadow with Judith Poole. Nor when she'd spread her sleeping bag on the metal springs and inserted the liner sheet after they'd warmed up Henry Lanyon.

Someone had tucked the gun inside her bag during the past few hours, here in the emergency cabin. But how? How and *when* had anyone managed to slip it into her sleeping bag without being detected? There were seven people in the cabin and *Helma* hadn't put it there. She began to rule out Ruth and Henry Lanyon, but having read that story about the dead man who wasn't dead after all, she lumped her friend and the injured man back in with Judith, Brentley, Whittaker, and BonBon.

Around her, she heard the rustles and creaks of the others settling into their sleeping bags and bunks, the crackling fire, and the rising whoop of the wind. A light snore like a gargle sounded from her left. She carefully pulled aside her space blanket and peeked into the shadowy room. One of her cabinmates had to know she'd discovered the gun as soon as she climbed into her bag.

Brentley Utterson, who'd offered to take the first watch of Henry Lanyon and to keep the fire going, slouched at the picnic table with his rounded back to her, reading a paperback book, his reddish hair glowing in the light of the kerosene lantern. Judith Poole lay on the bunk next to Helma, her sleeping bag pulled to her forehead, while BonBon slept on the top bunk above Judith, the nails of one manicured hand glowing in the lantern light.

Henry moaned and Brentley closed his book on his finger as he turned toward the ill man's bunk, already rising from the picnic table. The front of Brentley's head, his pate bare of hair, caught the shiny reflection of the lamp. Certainly there'd been thick hair growing there earlier.

She dropped the silver blanket before Brentley caught sight of her and returned to contemplating the pistol cradled on her lap. Why was it here?

Helma Zukas wasn't an expert but she knew a little about firearms, purely from research she'd conducted after finding herself in a situation where a firearm was pointed at her head. She'd always felt more confident if she were able to correctly label the items in her environment, especially during an emergency, when accuracy might prove vital.

And now, this ominously appearing gun, she guessed

from her past perusals of the *Shooter's Bible*, was a semi-automatic pistol. It was small, with a textured grip, hardly longer than her hand, androgynous, neither a man's gun nor a woman's, but one that might fit into either a pocket or a purse. It felt heavy, solid, as if it were loaded. She tentatively touched the magazine release on the grip, intending to check for cartridges in the magazine, then changed her mind and pulled her hand away. In the quiet cabin, she didn't dare; any or all of her mates might recognize the sound of the magazine opening.

She thought of Scotty and sniffed the barrel of the gun. Had it been fired recently? It smelled metallic, but she was unsure how it was supposed to smell. But Helma *was* certain of one fact: She wasn't spending the night with a pistol in her sleeping bag. She turned her head, searching around her sparse bunk for a niche to conceal the gun, but that would be like attempting to hide a flashing red light.

Above Helma, Ruth rolled over and the springs sagged downward beneath Ruth's hips. There was no way even to slip the gun beneath a mattress since the bunks weren't equipped with mattresses, only the dense mesh springs.

Finally, Helma's eyes settled on her backpack, which leaned against the foot of her bunk. For the moment, her pack was the only sensible hiding place, the one location where no one else was likely to stumble accidentally across the pistol—and where she could keep an eye on it.

She smoothly and silently reached for her pack and deftly opened the top compartment. Then, holding the gun by the grip, she slid it to the bottom and rear, beneath her wool socks and beside her sunscreen. That completed, she secured the flap and repositioned herself inside her sleeping bag—after carefully running her hands along its length to be sure there were no other hidden surprises.

She lay awake, sorting through reasons a hiker might carry a gun: hunting, protection, an off-duty policeman, but not coming up with any that made good hiking sense, especially considering that whoever owned the gun had passed it on to Helma. Why give it away if it was legitimately owned?

Helma Zukas finally drifted into a troubled sleep, positive she'd just closed her eyes when a hand on her shoulder rudely awakened her.

"C'mon, Helm. It's your friggin' turn."

Helma sat up, momentarily bewildered, checking the bedside for her digital clock which was safely at home in her apartment.

"It's your turn," Ruth repeated in a loud whisper, carefully enunciating each word. "Are you alive or what?"

"It's the heat in here," Helma whispered, unzipping her sleeping bag. "It makes me groggy."

Despite the cold and snow outside and the drafts that crept along the floor, the cabin *was* hot, the piney, slightly smoky heat of a fire kept going at full tilt.

"This place is all yours. Guard it well." Ruth placed a stockinged foot on the edge of Helma's bed, balancing there.

"Ruth," Helma began. "I found . . ." intending to tell Ruth of the gun, then realizing how audible their voices were in the silent cabin.

"What?" Ruth asked.

"How's Henry?" she asked instead as she pulled on her shoes and tied them after glancing at her backpack where the pistol rested.

"Restless. Wake up Whittaker if he gets worse. Whether he admits it or not, Whittaker has more training than he lets on."

"What about . . ." Helma began but Ruth waved her away, pulling herself up to her bunk on her stomach and disappearing over the top into a nest of loose clothes and a sleeping bag. "Just wing it," Ruth mumbled.

Someone, most likely Ruth, had left a half bottle of whiskey on the picnic table beside the burning kerosene lamp. Helma uncorked the bottle and sniffed the buttery charcoal odor. Like many foods and beverages with tastes she disliked, she found the odor of whiskey pleasant, stimulating even. She recorked the bottle and left it beside the lamp and quietly moved across the room to the window.

The snow continued, the flakes smaller in the colder night temperatures. The snow created its own pale light, forming wan shadows where it piled along fir branches, weighing them down until the wind blew just right and scattered the snow like powdered confetti, the boughs springing upward. There was no other movement, only snow, and Helma returned to the picnic table.

She sat on the hard bench, wondering if one of her cabinmates was watching her, curious what Helma thought of the gift he or she had left in the bottom of her sleeping bag. Instead of hiding the gun, did the giver suspect Helma might *need* a gun?

Helma distractedly flipped through Scotty's notebook, page by page, reading the dead man's brief notes: "Sunshine, 62°, Hyde Point." Nothing personal, just their itinerary ending abruptly at False Bridge on Jekyll Glacier.

"Look out!" Henry Lanyon suddenly cried out and Helma rushed to his bunk, feeling the man's forehead with the back of her hand at the same time she murmured calming phrases. His head was warm, feverish.

Henry opened his deep-set eyes but peered straight through Helma in such fixation she turned to look behind her. "The beach," he whispered. "I'd like to sit on the beach."

"Soon," Helma reassured him. "Just lie still now and rest."

"Did I pack my comb?" he asked, weakly patting the shirt pocket on his injured side.

The pocket of the shirt Whittaker had given him was empty but before Helma could think of a reassuring response, Henry lapsed into a fitful doze.

She sat beside him for a while longer, recalling an article she'd found for a library patron relating how those close to death were frequently concerned about travel tickets or packing their bags, all symbols of taking leave of the world. In a semiconscious corner of his mind, did Henry believe himself close to death?

She crossed the plank floor to Whittaker's bunk and leaned down beside him. His body stretched the length of the bunk and a few inches beyond. Whittaker's white blond hair was tousled, his eyes open. "Excuse me," she said softly.

"Yeah?" he asked. Expressionless, without surprise.

"Henry has a fever."

"Give him an aspirin," Whittaker said.

"And bother you in the morning?" Helma asked, noting the curly hair showing at the V-neck of Whittaker's t-shirt, the same color pale hair as on his head. "Can you examine him now?"

"No need to now," Whittaker said, turning over. "Later."

"But what if . . ." she began.

"In the morning," he repeated in a muffled voice.

Helma crushed an aspirin in water for Henry, and sat beside him while he gripped her hand and once mumbled, "No sauce on the steak, please," until she was certain his fever was holding steady. When she returned to the picnic table, Judith Poole was rising from her bunk, dressed in a blue jogging suit.

Judith put a finger to her lips and swiped her fingers through her gray hair with little effect. She sat down across the picnic table from Helma and rested her arms on the plank surface, chin cupped in her hands. "I heard him call out," she whispered, nodding toward Henry but her eyes intent on Helma. "Do you think he's going to die?"

"No," Helma assured her. "I don't."

"Does Whittaker?"

"I don't know."

"I've seen Whittaker before," Judith said.

"Where?" Helma asked.

"I don't remember where, but you don't forget a man who looks like that," she sighed, "like a Norse god."

"If you remember, will you tell me?" Helma asked.

"I will," Judith promised. "Henry would have died if you and Ruth hadn't found him."

"Probably."

"Then somebody would have had to search the mountains for his body," Judith said, a touch of eagerness in her voice as if she were looking forward to a companion on her annual mission.

"Did Henry wake you up or were you already awake?" Helma asked.

"I'm a light sleeper," Judith said proudly. "I wake up at the slightest noise, prepared to . . ." She stopped.

"Prepared to do what?" Helma asked.

Judith shrugged and folded her hands together. "Whatever needs to be done."

"I slept so soundly I didn't hear anyone else moving around," Helma told her. "Did you?"

"Of course. Everyone except you, and"—she nodded toward Henry's bunk—"got up at least once."

"They went outside?" Helma asked, glancing at the

shelf where they'd placed three of the flashlights, including Brentley's bright yellow two-in-one krypton flashlight. All were there.

Judith nodded and said in a confidential tone, "I don't think the men were gone long enough to go all the way to the amenities." She smiled sagely. "Men have an advantage over women in the wilderness."

"Do you have family or friends who help you hunt for Roger?" Helma asked Judith who was softly tapping her fingertips on the table, her eyes piercing. Her nails were short, clipped neatly close to the quick.

"Oh no. Just me. What little family I still have thinks I'm crazy, or at least an embarrassment." She shrugged. "But I don't care. Once you get far enough into the mountains, there aren't any rules anymore. That's why I like to come up here. You just do whatever you want and go where your feet lead you. I don't stay on the trails, of course. I won't find Roger by walking the trails."

"Don't you ever fear you're in danger?" Helma asked, attempting to work her way around to the subject of firepower protection.

Judith chuckled. "Certainly not. I'm not afraid of animals or falls, or . . ." She smiled. "Or even avalanches. I've studied them, you know. It would be a challenge to be caught in one." She cupped her hands around her face. "Try to do this if you're ever buried, before the snow settles, so you'll make more of an air pocket. You'll live if they can find you in thirty minutes. You don't just pop up out of an avalanche like people do in the movies. The snow above you hardens like concrete."

"I'll remember that," Helma said.

Judith held her cupped hands to her face for overlong, as if she were imagining ten feet of snow tumbling and settling above her body. Before Helma could continue her gun-tracking tack, Judith rose and said in distracted

chapter eleven

SNOW ON THE ROOF

When dawn broke, the wind had died down but in its place, accompanying the still falling snow, a strange band of mist hung in the air. It stretched through the trees and around the cabin, hovering a few feet above the ground and fifteen to twenty feet high, impenetrable as a dense cloud.

"It's like a ribbon tied around us," Judith commented. At least two feet of snow had fallen during the night, probably more. Since the wind had blown and sculpted the snow, it was impossible to tell.

"Or a snake," BonBon added, staring out the window, her hairbrush momentarily paused. "A boa constrictor."

Helma orchestrated an array of pots on the woodstove, filled with various forms of cooked cereal and reconstituted fruit, all of it cooking in liquid made from melted snow which Helma had boiled and purified with iodine tablets. Her own carefully rationed, packaged, labeled, and recorded meals were now part of the community stores.

And as she cooked, she carefully monitored the faces of her cabinmates, on the lookout for stealthy glances toward Helma's neatly folded sleeping bag where she'd found the pistol. Sooner or later the guilty person would give him or herself away: the guilty always did.

Less than ten minutes later, the band of mist was gone. Not a wisp of it remained, as if it had twisted sinuously away through the snowy mountains.

Brentley returned after a long trip to the amenities, smelling of cigarette smoke. "Maybe it'll clear off by noon," he said, dropping his Gore-Tex parka on his bunk.

"Do you usually hike alone?" Helma asked him, once again attempting to guide the conversation around to weapons, specifically handguns.

"Well, Helma, I usually have more hiking partners than I have time to hike," Brentley said as he buttoned the cuffs of another brand new flannel shirt. "This time I needed solitude." He gazed around the crowded cabin, shaking his head slightly and repeating, "Solitude."

"Until you met BonBon at the trailhead."

"That's right. I took pity on a lady all dressed up with nowhere to go."

"How kind of you," Ruth deadpanned.

"Yes, it was," Judith agreed with genuine warmth, and Brentley smiled and bobbed his head as if recognizing applause. Beneath his joviality, Helma noticed his narrowed eyes, the tense edge to his voice.

"But hiking alone?" Helma persisted. "Isn't it dangerous? How do you protect yourself?"

"*I* don't need protection," Brentley said. "Nothing up here I can't handle."

Ruth and BonBon sat beside each other at the picnic table, their hair pulled away from their faces, sharing BonBon's mirror while they artfully applied their makeup, BonBon's highlighted by tones of pink, Ruth's by black and purple. Ruth wore yesterday's wrinkled skirt and shirt while BonBon was dressed in a fuzzy pink and white sweater and tights.

"They've *got* to find us today," BonBon said. "This is such a waste of time."

Judith remained near the window, her gaze drawn into the snow again and again, turning her head in startled jerks as if she'd caught movement from the corner of her eye. "Weather at this altitude is unpredictable," she said gravely. "The snow could stop completely in an hour and the temperature rise to seventy or it could keep on like the winter of 1970-71. Over a thousand inches fell on Paradise in Mount Rainier National Park." She nodded in satisfaction, staring into the snow. "A lot of avalanches that year."

"I have an important meeting tomorrow," Brentley said. "It's vital I get out of here today."

BonBon looked up from her makeup case where she was extracting tubes of lipstick. "You told me you were hiking for a week."

"I forgot about this meeting," he said, not meeting BonBon's eyes, his jovial mood disappearing. "It means millions of dollars. I might have to risk it and hike out on my own."

"That would be inviting death," Judith told him.

Brentley shrugged and Helma noticed how his hands worked in his pockets as if he were used to jingling keys or coins when he was nervous.

"You might like to try this papaya blush stick," BonBon told Ruth. "With your skin tones it would be more flattering than that shade of plum."

"So what exactly is the unflattering effect of this shade of plum on my complexion?" Ruth challenged.

BonBon shrugged. "Youthful skin can handle deep shades more gracefully than . . . mature skin."

"I'm not into being graceful," Ruth said, slashing a

swath of plum across her cheek. ''I'm into being visible.''

''I was only trying to be helpful,'' BonBon said disdainfully, delicately dabbing papaya onto her own cheeks.

Every now and then Ruth or BonBon glanced speculatively at Whittaker, who knelt beside Henry's bunk, his pale head bent as he held a cup of liquid to the injured man's lips. Even without any show of compassion, Whittaker handled Henry with such ease and assurance, the others had gladly demoted themselves to his assistants.

To the women's disappointment, Whittaker rarely spoke except in response to comments made directly to him. His light blue eyes never settled for long on any of their faces and never once lit up with any emotion akin to interest, rather they remained gloriously indifferent and excruciatingly alluring.

''May I help you, Helma?'' Brentley asked, showing his teeth in a wide smile that stretched his mouth like a grimace. ''I'm a pretty good hand in the kitchen myself.''

Ruth raised her brows at Helma, then rolled her eyes and went back to the rigors of makeup application.

''Breakfast is under control,'' Helma told Brentley, ''but you might volunteer to cook lunch.''

''Oh, well, we'll see,'' Brentley said, backing away from the stove and joining Judith who'd moved to the picnic table.

''When do you think the rescuers will arrive?'' BonBon asked Helma as she stored her makeup away in a bright paisley case.

''That's impossible to say. It depends on the weather and where they're searching. There are thousands of square miles of forest up here.''

"Where there's life, there's hope," Brentley said in a voice that belied his words.

"I have hope, even without life," Judith said quietly. The red-haired man leaned across the table and patted her hand.

"You'll find Roger someday," Brentley said with all the sincerity of an adult assuring a child that Santa Claus really truly did exist and which Judith appeared to believe just as ardently.

"May we listen to your radio while we eat?" Helma asked Whittaker as she pushed the pots away from the heat and beckoned everyone to fill the various selection of bowls.

"Go ahead," he said without raising his head from Henry. "It's under my bunk."

The others ladled up breakfast from the pots on the stove. "No thanks," Helma heard BonBon say. "Breakfast is so fattening."

The radio sat on the plank floor beside Whittaker's well-worn hiking boots. His equally worn but expensive backpack lay crosswise on his bunk. As Helma picked up the transistor radio she couldn't help noticing how tightly packed Whittaker's contoured backpack was, even after the removal of his food and cooking utensils, just as Ruth had pointed out. Whittaker was packing far more equipment than anyone else in the cabin.

Helma carried the precious radio to the table and sat down next to Ruth, who was heartily spooning up her oatmeal and reconstituted peaches. They all silenced, watching Helma and the small black radio expectantly.

As curious as she was about the state of their rescue, Helma was burning to know why the Bellehaven Public Library had been mentioned during the radio news broadcast the night before. Could it have been the strike, or was it a slow news day and the library was receiving much deserved and overdue praise?

Helma clicked the dial at the side of the radio. Nothing happened. She turned the volume to its highest level, then moved the tuner button, searching for a station.

There were no droning voices, no rock music, no hysterical talk show hosts. And no static. The radio was dead.

"Did it work last night?" Helma asked Whittaker, who was mildly watching her futile efforts.

"I don't know. You were the last one to use it."

"Maybe you forgot to turn it off and the batteries ran down," BonBon offered. "That happened to me once—on the beach in San Diego. I was so mad."

"I hate it when that happens," Ruth said.

"I *know* I turned off the radio last night," Helma said, "because I had to turn it *on* just now."

"Check the batteries," Ruth advised as Helma was already prying off the battery compartment cover with the handle end of her camp fork.

The compartment was empty; the batteries were gone.

"Dum da dum dum," Ruth intoned. "A battery thief resides in our midst." She looked over at Whittaker. "Do you know anything about this? The radio was under your bunk."

He nodded his handsome head toward Helma, asserting again, "She was the last one to use it."

"The batteries were in the radio when I returned it to you," Helma said.

"Don't look at me," Whittaker said as they all looked at him expectantly.

"Somebody snuck the radio out from under Whittaker's bunk," BonBon said, "in the middle of the night."

"But when?" Judith asked.

"On a watch," Brentley said. "That's the only time any of us were alone. Whoever did it waited until the rest of us were asleep; it was right there in plain sight on the floor, right? He—or she—removed the batteries and then returned the radio without waking up a soul.''

''Well, I didn't do it,'' BonBon said.

''Me neither,'' Judith added.

''Ditto,'' Brentley agreed.

''So okay, none of us did it,'' Ruth said. ''Are we unanimous on that score?'' She glanced from face to face, accepting nods of agreement, then turned to Helma. ''Case closed.''

''That's absurd,'' Judith argued. ''Of course one of us took the batteries. I say we search all the packs.''

Helma replaced the battery cover on the radio's battery compartment, thinking of the gun stashed in her backpack. ''However it was done, the act has been completed,'' she said. ''There's no point in accusing one another or searching each other's possessions.'' She stood and set Whittaker's radio in the middle of the table. ''What's imperative now is that whoever has the batteries, return them immediately. This is not a time for juvenile antics. We are in a dangerous situation and the radio may save our lives.''

''Maybe that's the point,'' Ruth mumbled.

''What do you mean?'' BonBon asked.

''Whoever took the batteries,'' Ruth told her, ''would like to reduce the chance of our escaping this desolate cabin with our lives.''

BonBon sniffed. ''Well, *I* don't see that having a radio makes *any* difference in how soon we're rescued.''

''But don't you see something sinister in the batteries' disappearance?'' Judith asked. ''Now, when we need them most.''

''Not to me,'' Ruth said as she scooped the last of her breakfast from her bowl. ''That's the story of my life.''

''I believe you,'' BonBon told Ruth, smiling sweetly and touching her chin with a pink nail.

Ruth's eyes narrowed, then glinted, and Helma hastily said, ''Whether we have a radio or not, as soon as the weather clears, search and rescue helicopters will be looking for stranded hikers."

"Like I said," Brentley told them as he pushed away his empty bowl. "I have an important meeting tomorrow."

"The trail's probably obliterated until you get below the snow line," Helma told him.

"Then all I have to do is descend until I'm out of the snow," he said, smiling indulgently at Helma. "I've hiked these mountains before. Am I correct in believing this is your first mountain hiking experience?"

"I researched and read extensively before undertaking this outing," Helma told him.

"That's right," he said, his smile widening. "In the library. I noticed you brought a reference collection with you." He waved his hand toward Helma's small collection of books shelved on the floor beside her bunk. "You know, I used to work in a library."

"You said you sold real estate," BonBon interjected.

"Not just 'real estate,' " he corrected. He paused as if naming a rare and expensive wine, "Condos." He pointed to Helma. "You'd be happier in a condo than where you live now."

"How do you know where I live?" Helma asked.

"I can guess. An apartment, am I right? For years you've been throwing your money down a hole in rent. Nothing to show for it. Afraid to commit to buying a house."

"That's not all she's afraid to commit to," Ruth added. "Ask her about the chief of police."

"Too risky to buy a house, you think," Brentley went on. "And you're right. Houses can have electrical and plumbing problems, leaky roofs, yard upkeep. But a condo; now there's a nice compromise for a girl like you. Almost like renting but you've got yourself an investment, a tax deduction . . ."

"Which library did you work in?" Helma interrupted.

"University of Iowa," Brentley said, "while I was in the writing program."

Ruth's mouth dropped open, so Helma's didn't have to. "You?" Ruth asked. "You were at the Iowa Writers' Workshop?"

For the first time, an unprotected expression crossed Brentley's face: a flash of disillusionment and regret. Then it was gone, replaced by a sardonic grin. "A million years ago. Great parties, if you like associating with prima donnas. I saw the light and joined the real world."

"The batteries . . ." Helma began.

"Who has to do the dishes?" BonBon interrupted.

"Not Helma," Ruth said emphatically. "She cooked."

"But I didn't eat," BonBon said. She bit her lip and Judith offered, "I'll do them this morning. We can take turns."

"Yeah," Ruth told BonBon. "We'll put you last and maybe we'll be rescued before your turn comes up."

"I wish," BonBon said.

"For sure," Ruth countered.

"If we had a gun," Helma said, changing tactics from the missing batteries. Although she believed the two incidents were connected, she was disappointed to discover only rapt attention on the faces of her audience.

"What?" Ruth prompted. "You could make sure nobody did their dishes out of turn, or would you force whoever stole the batteries to confess?"

"No," Helma said, "but we might be able to shoot game to supplement our food."

"They're as hunkered down as we are," Brentley said.

"We have plenty of food," BonBon protested. "I couldn't eat anything we *killed*."

"A gun *would* be convenient," Helma tried again, this

time glancing over at Whittaker, who was staring blankly toward the window, obviously not listening. She'd hoped for a flinch, a shifting of eyes, the slightest expression of guilt, but none of her cabinmates seemed to find her comments on weaponry anything more than idle conversation, not nearly as interesting as the dishwashing schedule or the missing batteries. *Someone* was an excellent actor.

Beneath the rattle of Judith washing pots and plates in a collapsible plastic bucket on the picnic table, Ruth followed Helma to her bunk and whispered, "What's with the gun question?"

Both Judith and BonBon glanced their way, the dishwashing paused. In the tiny cabin, whispering was as attention-getting as shouting.

"Of course I have one," Helma said in a normal voice, handing Ruth her sewing kit. "You can give it back later," with the slightest emphasis on the word "later."

Ruth looked at the sewing kit in the palm of her hand as if it were an undesirable insect. "What . . ." she began. "Oh. That's right. I'll give it back *later*." Then she held up the sewing kit and turned to Judith and BonBon, snapping her bra strap through her shirt. "I'm coming apart," she announced.

"That doesn't happen if you buy better labels," BonBon said.

"I'd like to sew up her lips," Ruth muttered, climbing up to her bunk.

BonBon sat at the picnic table with one of Helma's laminated maps spread before her. "How high are we?" she asked Helma. "Where are we?"

Helma pointed out the X she'd marked in ballpoint on the plastic surface of her hand-prepared map. "Right here. Our elevation is approximately 5,700 feet.''

''And we came from here,'' BonBon said, tracing her finger down to the trailhead over two thousand feet lower. ''Do you think it's snowing there, too?''

''It may be,'' Helma said. ''Probably not as heavily as here.''

''How will they ever find us?'' BonBon asked in despair, smoothing her hands over the great expanse of the wilderness area.

Helma returned to her bunk and read a chapter titled ''The Pattern for Survival'' from one of the books she'd carried up the mountain. The chapter listed priorities in a cold weather environment: fire, shelter, food, signal. She flipped to the chapter on emergency signals. There was no use tramping out letters in the snow; it was too deep and still falling. They needed the heat from their stove too much to pile damp vegetation in it and cause smoke. There was no sunlight to reflect light from and who would see it anyway? They were in need of a signal that was more permanent.

Spread clothing against a contrasting background, her book advised. ''Is anyone wearing red?'' she asked the group.

''It's not a very popular color this year,'' BonBon said.

Blues, browns, greens. They all wore muted and natural colors, except for BonBon's pinks. Pink wasn't *that* much of a contrast against snow. Then Helma caught the look on Ruth's face. ''You're wearing red,'' she said.

''Why do you want to know?'' Ruth asked.

''We need a bright and contrasting color against snow.''

''Who in hell's going to see it?'' Ruth asked.

''We'll increase our chances,'' Helma told her.

''There's the flagpole outside,'' Judith eagerly suggested.

"But they're brand new," Ruth pleaded. "And they're pretty small."

"It's for the good of the group," Brentley said, his interest definitely rising.

"If whoever took the batteries confesses, I'll do it," Ruth said. No one stepped forward. Ruth groaned and said after a long-suffering sigh, "All right, damn it. Turn your backs, everybody."

Which they all did, until Ruth said, "I'm decent," and they turned to see Ruth holding out matching red lace bra and panties. "Go ahead. Run it up the flagpole."

Henry Lanyon's fever rose. He thrashed in his bunk, moaning when he jostled his shoulder.

"I think he's worse," Judith said, looking down at him.

"He needs a doctor," BonBon said, wringing her hands.

"Insulin," Helma said. "He could be slipping into a diabetic coma."

"But being a diabetic without insulin doesn't account for the rising fever, does it?" Brentley asked.

Henry's lips moved and Helma leaned close. "Blond," he whispered.

"I beg your pardon?" Helma asked.

And again he said the word, "Blond." That was all. His lips were swollen and cracked, the bruise on his face turning an ugly green.

"What did he say?" Judith asked.

"I'm not sure," Helma said.

Blond. Did he mean someone in the cabin? There were two blonds: BonBon and Whittaker. Or had he said, "Bomb"?

"Could you repeat that please?" Helma asked, bending low again. But he made no response.

Ruth picked up the aluminum cup Whittaker had left

on the floor and sniffed it, wrinkling her nose. ''What is this stuff, anyway?'' she asked Whittaker, who sat at the table playing solitaire.

''Something I put together for him,'' he answered, playing a queen of hearts on his king of clubs.

Ruth frowned. ''Eye of newt, tongue of toad?''

''Just a tonic to help his fever.''

''Go in which direction?'' she challenged.

Whittaker swept the seven piles of cards into one front-to-back mess and stomped to his bunk, dropping onto it with a thump that rocked the metal legs against the wooden floor. ''Take care of him yourself, then, if you want.''

Henry's unfocused eyes were red and wild, filled with panic. He turned his head from side to side, gripping the sleeping bag with his uninjured hand. He was definitely worse.

''We have to get him off the mountain,'' Helma said.

''Be reasonable, Helma,'' Ruth told her, smoothing back Henry's damp hair. ''It would take three or four of us to do it and we'd be in as much danger as he is. We'd all end up lost in a snowbank. None of us have the right clothes, either.''

''We'll wear layers of all our clothes,'' Helma said. ''Layers are warmer.''

''I'd do it,'' Judith said dreamily. ''I'm not afraid of dying.''

''Dying isn't the objective,'' Ruth told her. ''Fear would be a healthier response, I think.''

''Jennie?'' Henry asked. Then again, ''Jennie?''

''Jennie?'' Ruth repeated, frowning.

''I bet Jennie's his girlfriend,'' BonBon said. She sat beside the bunk and took Henry's hand in her own, wincing as he gripped and squeezed her smaller hand, soothing, ''Shh, shh, you'll see Jennie soon.''

Gradually Henry quieted, releasing his grip on

BonBon's hand until she slipped hers from his grasp and rose. "Even his hands are hot," she said.

Helma peered out at the falling snow, the day no brighter than when they'd eaten breakfast. "We'll need to make a litter to carry him down the mountain," she said.

"Judith must have something," Ruth said.

"Why?" BonBon asked.

"For Roger. What were you planning to do when you found Roger?" Ruth asked Judith. "Not leave him in the snow, I'd bet."

A horrified expression crossed Judith's face. "No. We can't . . . It's Roger's. Only Roger's."

"We can use my tarp to make a litter," Helma assured the agitated woman. "We'll construct it today so we're prepared to leave the moment the weather changes."

"We've already experimented with the tarp idea. Remember?" Ruth said, swishing her hands one over the other in mimicry of the tarp escaping down the glacier with Henry Lanyon inside.

"This time we'll fashion a litter that gives us better control," Helma said. Her mind raced. "With handles, and the ends sewn closed, and a safety tether. If we lay him on sleeping bags to protect his body, we can drag him over the snow without any further injury."

"*We* should be so lucky," Ruth commented.

Brentley harumphed and flexed his shoulders. "I can design the litter," he said. "I've had classes in adapting to severe conditions."

Helma had already envisioned the litter, imagined stitch and seam size and methods to attach the handles. It was *her* project. *Attempt to gently redirect the agitated patron's interests*, she'd learned.

"If you're familiar with these mountains," she told Brentley carefully, "it would be valuable if you mapped a route to most efficiently—and safely—lead us below the snow level."

"I'll help you," Judith offered Brentley. "I know these mountains better than . . . most people."

Brentley looked doubtful for a few moments until Ruth said, in a voice so sarcastic Brentley missed it, "We girls will do the sewing," and then he gave his assent.

Whittaker remained on his bunk, bent over a paperback book. Judith and Brentley huddled together, murmuring, heads together over Helma's map while Helma, Ruth, and BonBon sat near Henry and worked on the tarp. Using their flimsy sewing kits, they stitched multiple rows of seams with double strands of thread, again and again, testing each seam as they finished it, the bear bells jingling with their movements. Ruth's fingers were punctured and dotted with blood, BonBon's seams surprisingly straight and tidy.

"My grandmother taught me," BonBon explained. "She was old fashioned. She believed any girl could catch a husband if she knew how to sew a fine seam, darn a sock, and embroider a dish towel."

"*My* grandmother believed a woman's chances of catching a husband lay in different talents altogether," Ruth commented around her thumb, which was in her mouth as she sucked blood from another pin prick.

"And I'm sure you learned your lessons well," BonBon said.

From the picnic table, Brentley raised his head from the maps and said, "Meow."

Helma gave each person in the cabin swift penetrating glances. None of her cabinmates appeared guilty or acted suspiciously or even seemed terribly interested in the missing batteries. Their main emotion was the growing irritation with their mutual status as stranded hikers. According to her book, irritation was preferable to resignation, but had the author envisioned seven cranky people trapped in a one-car-garage–sized building?

"Oh, look!" Judith Poole suddenly cried out.

They all rose—even Whittaker—and looked where Judith pointed out the window.

The snow had stopped and the sun poured through a clear patch of blue sky, illuminating the white landscape, which glittered so brilliantly it was painful to look at.

Brentley threw open the door but none of them complained at the sudden frigid air. Above the cabin, Jekyll Glacier, which the last time Helma had viewed it had been a jagged mass of ice dotted with rocks and dirt and green crevasses, had now blended with the mountainscape, covered over by an untold amount of snow. To walk there now would be disastrous.

As they marveled at the morning's sudden brilliance, their hearts rising, in front of their eyes the clouds gathered together, the streams of sunlight disappeared, and flakes began to drift downward from the sky, growing thicker by the moment. Jekyll Glacier vanished and the snow returned like the lowering of a curtain.

"Eye of the storm," Ruth commented as Brentley wordlessly closed the cabin door and they dejectedly returned to their places in the cabin.

chapter twelve

FIRE IN THE FURNACE

Helma returned from the amenities, one hand on the guide rope strung by Brentley, and the other shading her face from both the stinging snow and the strange light that even without sunshine caused a painful throbbing at the back of her eyes. As the day progressed, the wind had picked up, spinning into swirls and eddies as if thousands of independent winds randomly charged through the mountains.

The air was filled with the whisper and swish of blowing trees in the nearby stand, the low whistles of the winds cornering around the cabin and over the uncertain terrain. The new-fallen snow drifted over the heavier, wetter snow that had fallen first, filling in the tracks she'd created just a few minutes earlier.

Just as Helma was thinking that the guiding rope between the two buildings was now a necessity in the zero visibility, it went slack in her hands. From taut to no tension at all.

She stopped in the blinding snow, disoriented. Then she tugged behind her. The rope was still attached to the amenities, but when she peered in front of her, she couldn't see even the outline of the cabin; her vision was filled with snow. Up, down, and all around. She pulled on the rope, hoping it had only loosened, but it came toward her effortlessly, looping through the snow, no longer tied to the post in front of the cabin.

Helma *wasn't* lost. If she hung onto the rope and stretched out its length, eventually she'd reach the cabin. And the snow itself might let up enough to expose the warm building. She raised her collar against the cold creeping down her neck—she hadn't bothered with a scarf for such a quick trip outside—and took two tentative steps along what she hoped was the snow-filled path. She wasn't about to call out. Not yet.

Step after floundering step through the deep snow, Helma became aware that she'd stumbled out of the path and was struggling through untracked snow. She reached the end of the rope, one hand in front of her like a blind woman, without meeting the walls of the cabin. Keeping the rope taut, she began working her way to the left, circling like a pencil attached to an old-fashioned school compass. As long as she held tight to the rope, she'd be all right.

"Helma," a voice called over the wind. "What on earth are you doing?"

Helma took two steps forward and bumped into Ruth huddled against the wall on the tiny porch in front of the cabin. She'd approached the building from the side; in another few steps she would have found it on her own.

"The rope came untied," she told Ruth, holding the end to her face to be sure it had come untied and not cut before she reattached it to the post, tying it in a square knot with her clumsy fingers.

"That's weird," Ruth said. Only her eyes and nose were visible between the twirls of a snow-spotted scarf that belonged to Helma.

"Yes, it is," Helma agreed. "It's freezing out here. Let's go inside."

"Tell me about the gun first," Ruth said, her voice muffled through the scarf. "What's that all about? Does one of our fellow inmates have a gun?"

Helma stood beside Ruth beneath the narrow overhang which gave little protection from the snow and winds whipping around the cabin. "I found a pistol in the bottom of my sleeping bag," she told Ruth.

Ruth pulled her scarf away from her mouth and bent lower. "In your *sleeping bag*? How'd a pistol end up in your sleeping bag?"

"I don't know," Helma said, "but the missing radio batteries may have a connection."

"We're jammed in this place like the proverbial sardines. You can't even walk across the room without stumbling over somebody's feet. I know more about the personal habits of the people in this cabin than I do about my own. How could anybody hide a gun—*or* steal batteries out of a radio—without ten other people seeing it?"

"Seven. There are only seven of us, not ten," Helma corrected her. "People often can't see what they don't expect to see." Her cheeks were growing stiff with cold and her words felt clumsy and sluggish.

"But in *your* sleeping bag?"

"It may have been the handiest."

"Yeah," Ruth conceded, tucking her hands beneath her arms. "You were the first one to spread your bag out and make camp. So whoever hid the gun didn't want anyone to discover he—or she—had it."

"That's what I believe," Helma agreed.

"Because they performed a dirty deed with that gun," Ruth went on. She stomped her feet. "So not only is one of our accidental friends a battery thief but a gun-toting battery thief."

"Except," Helma said, "if you wanted to make a gun disappear, would you hide it in someone else's sleeping bag? Wouldn't it make more sense to get rid of it permanently? Maybe throw it in the snow?"

"Or down the hole?" Ruth said, frowning. "Unless that person wanted to see you blamed for a gun-wielding crime."

"Or wanted me to have access to a gun. We have no information about any of these people," Helma told her. "Their pasts, or proclivities." She rubbed her cheeks with her gloved hands, barely feeling the rough wool.

"It's BonBon," Ruth said with certainty.

"She doesn't strike me as the gun-wielding type."

Ruth shrugged and rewrapped her scarf around the exposed portions of her face. "It's my policy to suspect whoever I like least. So my second guess would be Brentley, lorder-over of women."

"We may actually be discussing two people," Helma said. "A person hiding a gun and another who stole the batteries from the radio. And each may be unaware of the other."

"Whoever disabled the radio did it because they were afraid we'd hear something about them. Think. What were the criminal stories on the news?"

"The vitamin scam," Helma said.

"And whoever escaped from the halfway house. Was that a man or a woman?"

"I don't recall if the announcer gave a name."

Ruth rocked back and forth, pulling further inside her light jacket. "God, who or what else will come out of the woodwork before the helicopters arrive?"

The tips of Helma's ears were growing numb, despite her stocking cap. "We must stay observant of all activity in the cabin," she told Ruth.

"Whoever hid the gun is the person who shot Scotty," Ruth said.

Helma desperately wished she'd examined Scotty's wound more closely. "When Henry's conscious, he may be able to tell us who attacked him and Scotty."

"If he knows. You've got the gun, right?"

Helma nodded. "I do. I tucked it into the bottom of my backpack. And my fingerprints are all over it. I didn't consider that it might have been used in a crime."

"What other reason is there to hide it? But we're on top," Ruth said with confidence, excitement even. "The gun is in your hands. When we figure out who the bad guy is, just point it at him until the cavalry arrives."

The cabin door was suddenly flung open, causing Ruth to nearly tumble inside, and Brentley leaned out, a stocking cap over his hair. "Helma, Ruth. Are you two okay?"

"Just enjoying the weather," Ruth told him. "Care to join us?"

"No thanks. I was just checking." And he closed the door.

"See," Ruth said. "He's suspicious, afraid we're talking about him."

Helma brushed the snow from her shoulders and head. "He was only concerned, Ruth. That's natural."

"I think it's very peculiar that Brentley's suddenly eager to get off this mountain to attend a *meeting* he just happened to forget until now."

"He could just be anxious to leave the cabin," Helma suggested, although she agreed, having noted Brentley's nervous fidgets. "Maybe he's claustrophobic."

Ruth shook her head and wiped her nose on her sleeve. "I'm watching him. I have a feeling Brentley intends to make himself scarce before the rescuers come knocking on our door."

"We don't *know* Brentley's a criminal of any kind," Helma warned Ruth, thinking of how far Ruth frequently went in her convictions.

"Maybe not. Did you see all those new clothes he's wearing? He's no mountain boy. I'll keep an eye on him;

it'll give me something to do during my confinement." She sighed. "Although I'd rather keep *close* tabs on Whittaker, the ice prince."

Helma was freezing. "All right," she agreed. "Now let's go inside."

"No. Wait a couple of minutes or Brentley will believe we're coming in because he told us to."

"What do you care what he thinks?"

"I don't, but I'm not going to give him the satisfaction."

"Well, I'm cold and I don't care how satisfied he is," Helma said, reaching for the door latch.

"Traitor," Ruth accused her, staying exactly where she was.

As soon as Helma closed the cabin door behind her, she felt the tension in the small room. BonBon sat cross-legged on her top bunk, glowering, her pink cheeks even pinker with emotion, her lips a tight line.

Brentley and Judith Poole sat across the picnic table from one another, in an animated conversation about melatonin and hip replacements. Whittaker was in his corner, his head back against the wall and his book held so close to his face Helma doubted he could focus on a single word.

She removed her jacket and crossed the room to Henry's bunk. Although he didn't appear peaceful, he was asleep, his face flushed and his eyelids fluttering as if he were viewing a reel of bad dreams. She hoped sleep was a good sign, that this wasn't a coma. She was prepared to take him off the mountain. His situation was dire, but she hoped instead that the snow would cease and a big, noisy helicopter would drop out of the sky.

The tarp lay bunched on the floor as if it had been thrown there, and Helma glanced up at BonBon, who was scowling in satisfaction at the nascent litter. Helma examined it to be sure it had only been tossed to the floor, not damaged. Finding it sound, she carried it to her own bunk and smoothed it flat over her sleeping bag. It was slow going through the tarp's heavy material. They'd each already broken at least one needle from their sewing kits.

"You were outside talking about me, weren't you?" BonBon asked from her top bunk.

"No," Helma said shortly.

"Well, I don't like your friend Ruth, either," BonBon continued as if Helma had confirmed her suspicions.

A sluggish and out-of-place fly buzzed slowly past Helma's arm and she reached out to swat the biting pest.

"Don't," BonBon warned and Helma's first thought was the adage that BonBon wouldn't hurt a fly.

Helma arrested her swat in midswing and watched spellbound as BonBon turned from morose to avid stalker. Her eyes following the fly, she stealthily and sleekly descended from her bunk and proceeded hot on its trail, her hands cupped in front of her.

BonBon, in all her pinkness, shadowed the fly between the bunks and around the picnic table, and then, near the stove, with a dart worthy of the most agile lizard, she flashed forward and imprisoned the fly in her cupped hands, smiling triumphantly.

"It's a deer fly," she said, peeking into her cupped hands. "Poor thing. I'll bet this weather was a surprise to her."

"How do you know it's a female?" Helma asked.

BonBon opened her hands where the deer fly perched on the hump of her right thumb as if it knew it was in the hands of an admirer. "A female's eyes are separated at the back," she said. "See? The male's meet. It's the female who does most of the biting. She's tough."

To see BonBon in her pink clothing, perfect makeup, and unchipped manicure admiring a fly was perplexing, to say the least.

"Entomology is a hobby of mine," BonBon explained.

"Entomology?" Helma repeated in surprise. "Entomology is your *hobby*?"

"Mm hmm," BonBon murmured, raising her hand and squinting at her tiny guest. "These guys can fly fifty miles an hour. Imagine the carnival ride that would be for us. Comparatively, I mean."

"Did you study entomology in college?" Helma persisted as BonBon twisted her hand, viewing the deer fly from every angle, glad Ruth wasn't inside to hear *this*.

"No. Art appreciation. My parents said if I studied the sciences I'd turn mannish."

"And you believed them?" Helma asked.

"Back then I did," BonBon said, shaking her head at the memory. She carried the fly to the small window farthest from the stove and set it on the sill, nudging it toward a crack in the wall, saying, "Better take a nap, honey."

As Helma regarded her, still pondering this unexpected facet of BonBon, Ruth finally came in from the cold, her lips blue, a humpy cap of snow on her head. She shrugged out of her coat and scarf beside the stove, snow landing on the cast-iron stovetop and skittering across the surface before it vaporized.

"Cold?" Brentley asked politely but without any real interest.

"Not bad," Ruth told him, her teeth chattering.

Helma noticed Whittaker watching Ruth over the top of his book, his expression intent but indecipherable.

The glacier groaned and they glanced uneasily at one another. The deep rumble was more of a feeling in Helma's chest than a sound.

Suddenly, apropos of nothing, Brentley asked Helma, "Supposing a patron requested a detailed overview of

Marxism, but not a whole book on the subject, where would you send him?"

Caught off guard, calling forth her formidable skills without contemplating what she might be getting herself into, Helma answered, "That depends on whether the patron was a student or an adult. The *International Encyclopedia of the Social Sciences* would be a good place to start. It reflects excellent scholarship from the 1930's."

"What if he wanted the plot to *For Whom the Bell Tolls*?"

Again, Helma answered without thinking, "*Masterplots*," and then seeing the challenging expression on Brentley's face, she realized this exchange possessed the possibility of escalating into a library showdown. "Where would you have looked?" she asked, remembering Brentley's claim to have worked at the University of Iowa library.

"The same," he said smugly, while Helma resisted the urge to offer other reference alternatives to his hypothetical patrons. Although she didn't stop herself from saying, "The library world has changed. Many of the references you were accustomed to years ago have now been replaced by computer services and on-line networks." Helma noticed how Brentley's smugness slipped when she slightly emphasized the words "years ago."

An aura of irritation hovered about the inhabitants of the cabin. Nothing was outwardly said or acted upon, but it was apparent in annoyed faces when Ruth knocked over a pot, or narrowed eyes when Judith began describing the mechanics of a slab avalanche again—"Once an avalanche gets moving, they can crash down the mountain at 200 miles per hour,"—and when Brentley suddenly announced into the silence, "I drive a Porsche, a white convertible."

Helma had an idea. "Why don't you lead us in a series of exercises, BonBon?" she asked, only to be met by groans from every corner of the room.

"No thanks."

"You've got to be kidding."

Accompanying the irritation, a curious lethargy held them all captive, as if their bodies had gained so much weight, any movement was too wearying. One after another, each yawned in jaw-cracking stretches and slumped into silence.

So, as if by assent, the weary cabinmates retreated to their bunks after lunch and settled in for long winter naps.

The snow still fell, thicker if that were possible, giving the sounds inside the cabin an underwater quality, like plugged ears. Sleep felt like the proper course, Helma thought, as long as the cabin stayed warm and they didn't stray into oblivion.

"I think it's time to hibernate," Helma heard BonBon say drowsily from her bunk before she drifted off.

Helma wasn't sure how long she'd been wrapped in an eerie dense slumber that cushioned her like a cocoon, when she grew aware of movement at the end of her bunk. She struggled awake, her eyes sticky with moisture, seeing first the drape of her space blanket and then turning toward the bottom of her bed.

And there, Ruth pawed through Helma's backpack, rooting around in it like a raccoon. Helma's carefully arranged supplies spilled from the top compartment, clean shirts mixing with toiletries, her comb lying on the bunk. When Ruth realized that Helma was sitting up and staring at her, she put her finger to her lips.

"What are you doing?" Helma mouthed.

Ruth shaped her right hand into a gun, then pointed to Helma's backpack and shook her head, pantomiming that there was no gun in Helma's backpack while Helma knew that was exactly where she'd put the pistol: at the rear of the top compartment, between her socks and sunscreen.

Helma never participated in games of charades so she resignedly climbed from her bunk and knelt beside Ruth and her pack, reaching inside to exactly the spot where she knew the gun was located.

It wasn't there. She felt beneath the plastic bottle of sunscreen, shoved aside her socks, bungee cords, and extra bottle of water purification tablets, then progressed to the lower compartment, doubting the gun would be there. It wasn't.

"I told you," Ruth said aloud, her voice exploding into the quiet cabin. "It isn't there."

Immediately from around them came stirring: waking gasps, rustling sleeping bags. Even wounded and ill Henry groaned.

"What isn't there?" Brentley asked, sitting up and placing rag-wool-stockinged feet on the floor, one hand adjusting his hair.

Without missing a beat, Ruth answered, "Helma told me she'd packed an extra scarf, but it's not here." She sat back and let Helma's pack fall against the bunk frame with a thump. "Oh well, it wouldn't have been my style, anyway."

Helma reclosed the compartments of her backpack, feeling the eyes of everyone in the cabin, coldly aware one of them was playing a dangerous game with her.

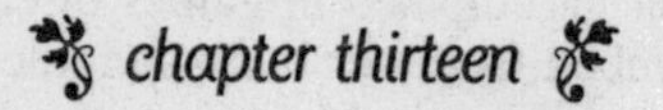

HIGH STAKES

"Oh, here they are!'' BonBon suddenly sang out while Helma still knelt beside Ruth, her hands in her backpack vainly searching for the mysterious gun.

BonBon pointed at an aluminum drinking cup in the middle of the picnic table, nearly jumping up and down, her sleepy smile wide.

''The batteries,'' Judith said, rising from her bunk and leaning over the table. She searched from face to face. ''They're here. Somebody has returned the batteries.''

''That's *my* cup,'' Brentley said, joining them as he tucked in his shirt over his rounded belly. ''Who put them in *my* cup?''

''Who had the opportunity?'' Judith asked.

''Everyone,'' Ruth said.

''Including you,'' BonBon told Ruth. ''You were the first one to get up. I saw you.''

''You're right,'' Ruth agreed. ''I was. But *you* found them. You could have just slipped these alkaline babies in the cup and then pretended you spotted them first.''

''Hah,'' BonBon said, curling her lip and saying in that smart way, ''As if.''

''At least the batteries have been returned,'' Helma

said. "The rest of us appreciate that, and now we can listen to the radio again."

Whittaker, who still sat on his bunk, leisurely reached for the radio and handed it to Helma. "This seems to be of most interest to you," he said, then rose and sauntered to Henry's bunk where he'd once again taken over as Henry's caregiver. Helma watched Whittaker's easy, graceful walk. "Blond," Henry had said. Whittaker was definitely blond.

She pried off the back of the radio and inserted the two AA batteries, matching positive to positive and negative to negative, then clicked on the dial.

The two stations, Canadian and Bellehaven, came to life, the cheerful voices entering the cabin like magic, although as high as Helma turned the volume, the sound didn't even approach conversation level.

"The batteries are wearing down," Judith observed. She glanced at her watch. "The news is on in twelve minutes."

Helma turned off the radio again. "We'll save the batteries until then," she said.

They waited, still logy and yawning, checking their watches, glancing speculatively outside at the continuing bad weather and at one another, warily alert to each other.

Under cover of Brentley's explanation of the wonders of amortization to Judith, Ruth whispered to Helma, "Are you sure the g-u-n was in your pack in the first place?" spelling the word as if no one else in the cabin would understand.

"Of course," Helma said in a low voice, holding up the blue tarp/litter and pretending to show Ruth a seam. "I placed it in the top compartment myself."

"This place could be haunted. Judith's Roger could be lurking under the beds and jerking us around. Have you thought of that?"

"Frankly, no," Helma said.

The litter to transport Henry Lanyon was finished, all its seams tautly sewn, fabric handles firmly attached, including Helma's safety feature: the forty-foot rope tied securely to one of the handles. There'd be no runaway tarps this time. The litter lay spread across the picnic table in all its blue glory and gay multicolored seams, a cheery little life raft.

"You did a good job," Brentley said, momentarily in a more relaxed mood. "Even I wouldn't be afraid to ride in it."

Even Whittaker grunted in approval, tugging on the straps and finding them sound. "Where'd you learn to secure material like this?" he asked, pointing to the corners joined by laces and rosettes of cloth.

"It's a concha," Helma said. "I learned it from the cards that used to come between layers of shredded wheat. My older brother collected them."

Brentley slapped his forehead. "Straight Arrow! I remember. Each card gave directions for a different Indian craft."

"Who's Straight Arrow?" BonBon asked, frowning at Brentley and Helma. "Is he on TV?"

"Wait," Ruth suddenly said, holding up her hand. "Nobody move. I forgot I've got my camera. Let's record this for posterity."

Ruth dragged her battered and ancient Nikon from her backpack, untangled it from a black bra, and fussed with the flash attachment while they all waited. Whittaker began to slink toward his bunk. "Not another step," Ruth warned him. "Come spring this could be the only evidence they find that you lasted this long. Everybody move over beside Henry so we can get the whole group."

Helma disliked the artifice of posing for a photograph, or the way photographs minimized reality, but she stood between Judith Poole and BonBon, realizing what Ruth was up to, the three of them holding the bright blue litter in front of them like a flag, Helma struggling to keep her smile from deteriorating into a grimace. A photograph of the group could be valuable to the law if the gun situation wasn't clarified before they were off the mountain.

The flash on Ruth's camera snapped like lightning, a shock of yellow in the white snowlight, and they all blinked and groaned and let out their held breaths. Ruth glanced at Helma, lowering one eye in a slow wink.

"One minute to news," Brentley said, and as one, they gathered around the picnic table.

Helma turned up the sound, which seemed even softer than the last time and hoped the batteries would hold out until they were rescued.

First the jingle, then the deejay asked over the fading theme music, "What do you think of this rain, Radio Land? It sure caught me with my windows down."

Helma glanced out the window where the snow continued to fall with the same relentless intensity.

The missing hikers had climbed the news ladder to the second top story, following the resignation of a city council member caught by a citizen's video camera as he left a local adult store, his arms laden.

"Eleven hikers are still unaccounted for in the mountains, trapped by a freak snowstorm," the announcer said in a deep and serious voice. "Search and rescue brought down eight yesterday and continue their search for the others, hampered by continuing bad weather."

"Eleven," Ruth said, glancing around the room. "And seven of the eleven are right here. That means four more hikers are sitting out this weather somewhere."

"We hope," BonBon said and Ruth nodded, her face serious in agreement.

The newscaster's voice raised in timbre, as if he were tacking on an anecdotal story to temper the serious tale of missing hikers. "And now for news from your local library. Negotiations have broken down between the staff and management and the library's currently being run with severely limited services. They're not taking phone questions, so don't call and ask them to solve your crossword puzzle stumpers."

Helma picked up the radio as if to draw more information from the man, but he went on to the story of the missing so-called "vitamin kings" and the rain-dampened soapbox derby.

It had happened. The paraprofessional staff had carried out its threat and gone on strike. Who was running the library? Ms. Moon and which librarians were attempting to run the state's busiest library *alone*? Chaos had obviously descended on Bellehaven. And here Helma Zukas sat, a mile higher and miles away from Bellehaven and her library, imprisoned by a snowstorm with an injured man and an edgy, cantankerous group of stranded hikers.

She distractedly turned off the radio and refolded the blue litter, setting it on the floor against the wall. Then she faced her cabinmates. "I think we should attempt to leave in the morning," she announced, "even if the snow doesn't let up."

Everyone's gaze shifted to the feverish Henry Lanyon, who still tossed in dreamlike agitation but with weaker, more tentative movements.

"I'm game," Brentley said. "I have that meeting I told you about—important. Why not leave this afternoon?"

"Count me in," Judith quickly added, smiling at Brentley. "The snow will be the most stable in the morning. That's the best time to travel in these conditions."

"It'll give us more daylight, too," Helma said. "What about you, Whittaker?" she asked.

"If I don't leave sooner," he said.

"We need you," Helma told him. "You're the strongest of the group." Brentley's face darkened at that comment; he raised himself taller, stretching his neck and squaring his shoulders. "We need everyone," Helma assured her comrades.

"Shouldn't somebody stay here?" BonBon asked. "In case they come to rescue us?"

"Nobody knows we're here," Brentley pointed out.

"They'd expect *somebody* to be here," BonBon persisted. "This is an emergency cabin. It would only be logical."

"We'll leave a note," Helma told her.

BonBon furrowed her brow prettily and blinked her large blue eyes. "We could divide up. You know, the . . . younger of us go down the mountain with Henry"—here she nodded to Whittaker and pointed to herself—"and the others wait here to be rescued. I mean, wouldn't that be fastest?"

"We old folks will do our best to keep up," Ruth said. "If we lag behind, you can shoot us and eat our flesh to survive."

"That's disgusting," BonBon said and flounced to her bunk.

Whittaker shook his head and added two more logs to the fire. He noticed Helma frowning at the diminishing stack of firewood and said, "There's enough wood outside for a couple more days. If we each bring in an armload when we go out . . ." He closed his mouth as if cutting off all thought of offering aid to the group.

"That's a good idea," she said, but his face had gone blank, as if he couldn't hear her.

Ruth stood beside the picnic table, hands on hips and lower lip between her teeth, watching Whittaker speculatively, a slight frown on her face, the beginning of a glint in her eye. Helma had seen it happen before. When a man didn't respond to Ruth the way she anticipated or felt she deserved, her next move was to bedevil him until he was so confused all he longed for was escape.

"Maybe we could read aloud," Helma said to Ruth. "Did you bring any books?"

Ruth jerked, aroused from contemplation. "That's your department. What did *you* bring?"

"Only a few necessary volumes."

Before Helma could stop her, Ruth was kneeling on the floor beside Helma's bunk, going through the books Helma had stood side by side against the bunk leg. "Let's see," she said. "What does a librarian consider necessary reading on a three-day hike?"

Ruth set Helma's books one on top of the other on her bunk, reading off the titles. "Wildflower identification: sweet. Forest ecology, first aid, short stories. *Birds and Mammals of the Cascades*. No dictionary? No eenie beanie set of encyclopedias like those tiny Bibles? No Shakespeare?" She searched around Helma's bunk. "Where's that little brown book you keep peeking at?"

"Aha!" she said, pulling a beige paperback from under Helma's sleeping bag and squinting at it. "What's this? It looks official." She glanced up at Helma. "An army field manual, Helma?"

Helma leaned forward and removed the paperback from Ruth's hands. "It's a cookbook," she said, unaccountably lying although there *were* a few recipes included in the manual; desperate recipes employing items like grasshoppers and tree roots and sprouting cattails. The actual title of the book was *Survival, Evasion, and Escape*, an army manual for soldiers caught behind enemy lines.

Ruth, who could easily read the title of the book, looked at Helma long and hard, then ran her hands through her bushy hair. "We need to know this, huh?"

"Perhaps," Helma said. She'd brought the book because it was full of succinct wilderness tips unencumbered by lyricism, with a decent index. She tucked the little book beneath her sleeping bag again. That morning she'd marked two chapters with Bellehaven Public Library bookmarks: one on cold-weather survival and the other on maintaining the will to survive.

"Well, I don't feel like reading," Brentley said. "Anybody else?"

"No thanks."

"No way."

"Forget it."

Ruth leaned over and whispered to Helma, "Have you noticed the May, December romance blooming right beneath our noses? Poor Roger may be iced forever." Helma glanced over in time to see Brentley gently nudge Judith's shoulder with his knuckle, suggestive of a caress.

Ruth sighed and glanced at BonBon, who'd climbed back on her bunk and was staring at Whittaker. "Do you think we'll deteriorate into fighting over the men, like those kids shipwrecked on that island?"

A diversion, the group needed a diversion before it deteriorated into factions, each of them challenging the other for higher and higher stakes, cooperation disintegrating into anarchy.

Ruth and Helma had been friends since they were ten years old, a friendship as puzzling as it was loyal. But even so, they'd rarely spent more than a few hours together, let alone *days*. And Helma admitted to herself that friendships were definitely easier to maintain when people didn't live in each other's pockets. She briefly wondered if marriages worked the same way.

Helma Zukas disliked games and hadn't played any since grade school but if ever there was a time when a game had its place, this was the moment. The afternoon stretched before them: white and shadowless and close. Seven bodies enclosed in a room comfortable for three or four. Seven people who wouldn't have chosen each other's company under the best of circumstances.

She quickly thumbed through *Survival, Evasion, and Escape* to the section titled, "The Will to Survive." The little book recommended nourishing the sense of humor, along with full participation in group activities. She supposed "full participation" could be interpreted as a suggestion that she for once gracefully engage in competition.

Helma glanced around the silent and sullen group, the only friendly interaction taking place between Brentley and Judith, and even that was edgy. Brentley was unable to sit still, his gaze moving between his companions and the window. The others sat on their bunks surrounded by imaginary lines like siblings defending their portions of a shared bedroom.

"Does anyone know how to play Botticelli?" Helma asked, the only mental game she could think of besides charades.

"What's that?" BonBon asked with a slight spark of interest, leaning over her top bunk, a nail file in her hand.

"One person thinks of a famous person. For example, I think of Benjamin Franklin. The rest of you ask questions. Judith might ask what kind of weather my character would be and I'd say 'lightning storm,' and Ruth might ask what kind of dog my character would be and I might say, 'Boston terrier,' until we've built up an image of Benjamin Franklin."

"I don't get it," BonBon said.

"Too cerebral, Helm," Ruth commented from her bunk above Helma where she lay flat on her back staring at the ceiling.

"Helma," Helma corrected. "Then how about if we tell stories?"

"Are you running for camp counselor?" Ruth asked.

"I was searching for a way to pass the time," Helma told her.

Ruth sat up and pointed to Whittaker. "I know! You have cards, Whittaker, right?"

Whittaker nodded from his corner bunk.

"Then let's play poker."

Even Whittaker brightened at that idea and Brentley began clearing off the picnic table, saying, "Poker, good idea."

"My little brother taught me how to play poker," BonBon said eagerly. "What'll we use for chips?"

"Matches," Brentley supplied. "Between all of us, we must have a few hundred."

Judith bowed out. "I'll sit with Henry," she said. "The rest of you go ahead."

"Five-card draw, jokers wild," Ruth said, swinging onto the floor from the top bunk. "Great idea, Helma."

"It was your suggestion," Helma said.

"Only the particulars. You had the generic."

"I don't know how to play poker," Helma told her. "I'll watch."

"No way. This is a group effort."

Full participation in group activities, the survival book had recommended. Enthusiasm. Helma sighed. "I'd only slow you down."

"All the more booty for the rest of us," Brentley said, emptying out Judith's matches and adding them to the growing pile on the picnic table.

"Mine are the waterproof ones with green tips," BonBon said. "I want them all back after the game."

"Only if you win them back," Brentley told her.

The air in the cabin was charged with sudden enthusiasm as they seated themselves around the picnic table.

Whittaker shuffled cards, Brentley remembered a bag of peanuts in his backpack, Ruth brought out a half bottle of whiskey and BonBon set a half-empty box of mints on the table.

"I really don't know how to play," Helma warned them again, hoping that poker was a game where players were able to lose and bow out judiciously soon.

Three hours later, BonBon and Judith stood at the stove concocting a late dinner from the store of provisions while Ruth and Whittaker hovered over Helma and Brentley, the last two players in the poker game.

Brentley's face was calm but a sheen of sweat glistened above his eyebrows. His eyes shifted between Helma and his hand.

"I recognize your wager and increase it by five," Helma said, pushing five green-tipped matches from her sizable store into the center of the table.

"It's 'I'll see you and raise you five,' " Ruth said in exasperation.

"Shh," Whittaker warned. "You're breaking their concentration."

"I'll see your five," Brentley replied, pushing his own matches into the pile with a flourish. Having done that, he leaned back, his face confident.

They eyed one another and Brentley said, "Read 'em and weep," spreading his hand of five cards on the table. "Four kings," he said smugly, reaching toward the pot.

Helma calmly laid her five cards in front of her: all diamonds, beginning with a ten and ending with an ace. "I'm calling the joker a king of diamonds. What's that called, a royal blush?"

Ruth clapped her hands and whooped. "Not blush: flush, a royal flush, and it beats four of a kind all hollow. Do you know what the odds are against a royal flush?"

Brentley pulled back from the pot of matches and hit

both fists against the table top. ''Damn right,'' he swore. ''Give me a break.''

''Lighten up,'' Ruth told him. ''Chalk it up to beginner's luck if that'll make you feel any better.''

''I've never seen a beginner have quite so much good fortune,'' Brentley replied. He faced Helma, his face reddening. ''Nobody has that kind of luck . . .''

Helma quit arranging her stack of matches so all the burnable ends faced away from her and rose to her feet. ''Are you accusing me of cheating?''

He stood, too, and pointed to her cards lying face up on the table, her royal flush. ''It's pretty unusual for a beginner to get a hand like that.''

''I do not engage in deceptions,'' Helma said in her silver-dime voice.

''She doesn't even wear mascara,'' Ruth said.

Even as she stood in the cabin in the midst of a snowstorm facing down a red-faced Brentley Utterson across the picnic table, Helma remembered a movie she'd seen as a child where a similar quarrel between two cowboys ended in a blazing and deadly shootout and she hoped that Brentley wasn't the person who'd removed the pistol from her backpack.

Whittaker lazily reached out one big hand and nudged Brentley's shoulder, only a light tap but it was enough to knock Brentley to the side, forcing him to stumble and catch himself. ''Cool it,'' Whittaker said, his voice deadly cold.

If Brentley had been a rooster he would have ruffled and bobbed and scratched. Instead, he grabbed his jacket and departed into the snowy evening while Judith stood at the stove watching him, her hands over her mouth and her eyes wide.

chapter fourteen

FEVERISH BREAKS

The bonhomie first generated by the poker game was long gone, the only positive outcome of that brief foray into gaming being that if the economy of the stranded group were based on matches, Helma was the undisputed woman of substance.

Only Helma sat at the picnic table to eat her reconstituted dinner; the others had chosen their bunks, dining in stiff silence that was interrupted by metal utensils against dishes or gusts of wind assaulting the little cabin.

Ruth and BonBon made little sniffing sounds whenever they caught each other's eye, their animosity prodded to the danger zone when BonBon suddenly turned to Ruth while they were sorting out dinner and said, "I know you were the one who put the batteries in Brentley's cup." To which Ruth replied, "It took me a while to find them in your little pink backpack. All those creams and makeup."

Even Brentley and Judith had separated, Judith gently troubled by Brentley's fit of bad manners over Helma's good luck at poker.

Helma read a page in her survival and evasion manual about "recognizing the onset of a passive outlook" and its dangers but refrained from suggesting any other diversions, wondering if Whittaker had the right attitude after all: silence was preferable to flare-ups and sullen standoffs.

After dinner, Helma waited until two minutes to six before she turned on the transistor radio, noting with a sickening feeling that the sound was even weaker than the last newscast. No one commented but she felt their alert attention as the faint theme music broke the silence.

The lost hikers were finally the rightful top story. "Two of the missing hikers walked out near Lyme Campground," the announcer said, "both suffering from severe frostbite. A volunteer search party organized by Mountain Rescue set out for the mountains this afternoon, joining other ground search efforts to find the remaining nine hikers until a break in the weather allows helicopters to fly, according to Ward O'Reilley. The snow level's currently at thirty-five hundred feet."

"Ward O'Reilly," Ruth repeated from her bunk, dropping her head into her hands. "We're doomed. We're going to die up here."

"Thirty-five hundred feet," Brentley said. "It won't be as long of a walk out as I thought."

Helma ignored both of them, leaning over the radio to catch the next story. "And now we turn to the library stand-off," the news broadcaster was saying with a touch of unnecessary humor. "After negotiations collapsed between staff and management, the mayor asked the Friends of the Library organization to take up the slack left by the striking staff." Here a clip of the mayor was played, sounding like Winston Churchill. "The library is this community's heart," he declared. "Its lifeblood. I will not allow it to be stricken and fail."

"It's like calling out the National Guard," BonBon commented.

The Friends of the Library, who ran book sales and

collected donations, vigorous supporters of the library, had never doubled as employees. ''This is against the union contract,'' Helma said. She turned off the radio as the announcer began a story about the vitamin scandal and looked out at the darkening sky, saying with rekindled resolve, ''I must return to Bellehaven. We leave at first light.''

''I thought we'd already decided that,'' Brentley said, glancing at Helma as if he believed she'd tricked him again.

''We know, we know,'' Ruth said wearily to Brentley, lifting her head from her hands. ''You've got an important meeting that can't go on without you.''

''That's absolutely correct.''

''What did you mean when you said we were doomed because that Ward guy was leading Mountain Rescue?'' BonBon asked Ruth.

''Just keep your fingers crossed he doesn't know I'm one of the missing,'' Ruth said.

''Why?'' Helma asked.

Ruth made fists and pushed them beneath her cheekbones. ''Remember my city hall paintings?'' she asked Helma.

''He was one of those you depicted?''

''Mm hmm, the one with the . . .''

''Don't tell me,'' Helma warned her. ''But that doesn't matter, Ruth. The rescue teams are beyond politics.''

''Says you.''

''We'll be out of here before they show up, anyway,'' Brentley said. He wasn't jingling imaginary coins or keys in his pockets anymore; now he'd taken to rubbing his thumbs over his fingertips in a continuous jittery movement, accompanied by a barely perceptible rocking of his upper body.

''You're a little jumpy, aren't you?'' Ruth asked, gazing down at him from her bunk. "Eager to get out of here?"

"Aren't you?" Brentley asked in turn. "Aren't we all?" He waved an arm around the cabin, his thumb and fingers rubbing, rubbing. "This place would drive a saint crazy."

"Never met one," Ruth replied.

"Is there anything to drink?" a voice suddenly and reasonably asked.

Judith gasped. Ruth announced, "A miracle," and BonBon jumped lightly to the floor from her bunk and knelt beside Henry's bed. "Hello," BonBon said, smoothing back the injured man's brown hair. "We found you hurt on the mountain and we've been taking care of you. Do you feel better?"

Henry closed his eyes and said, "Water?"

"I'll get it," Judith said, bustling to the pots and pans on the stove.

Helma placed the back of her hand against Henry's forehead. It was damp but cool. "His fever has broken," she said.

From his bunk, Whittaker nodded with only the slightest smirk of self-righteousness.

"I guess your magic potion worked after all," Ruth told him.

"I guess so," he said and returned to his book.

Judith held out a sierra cup half filled with water.

BonBon took the cup and held it to Henry's lips, solicitously murmuring and coaxing the pale man with a nursing tenderness she hadn't exhibited prior to that moment.

"Put a little life back in a man and he looks a lot more interesting, doesn't he?" Ruth asked her, smiling as BonBon shot her a deadly look.

Henry winced and Helma asked him, "Is it your

shoulder that hurts most? Can you describe your injuries?''

He laid his head back against Judith's folded jacket, which formed his pillow. ''Shoulder,'' he said in a weak and raspy voice, gazing at the circle of faces gathered around his bunk, and with his left hand, touched his abdomen. ''Something here.'' With difficulty he turned his head and peered around the cabin. ''Where's . . .''

''Scotty,'' Ruth supplied. ''He . . .'' She stopped when she saw Helma shaking her head. ''What happened up here? How were you injured?''

''I'll tell you,'' he said, and then, as if he'd expended too much effort, Henry nodded briefly and closed his eyes.

''Now that his fever's down, isn't it safer to wait here for help?'' Judith asked.

''Not when he needs insulin,'' Helma said.

''Insulin,'' Henry murmured.

''Do you remember when you last shot up?'' Ruth asked.

''He probably has no idea how much time has passed,'' Helma told Ruth. To Henry she said, ''When you're off the mountain, buy yourself a bracelet or a necklace stating you're a diabetic. What if we hadn't found the card in your pocket?''

He nodded again and reclosed his eyes.

''Save the chastising for later,'' Ruth said. ''You're exhausting him.''

Helma opened her notebook to the tabbed section marked ''Statistics.'' ''Sunrise is at 6:44 tomorrow morning,'' she said. ''We'll leave at seven o'clock.''

''Aye aye,'' Brentley said, saluting Helma with one finger to his forehead.

''Got a better idea?'' Ruth asked him.

Brentley shrugged and went back to rearranging the

contents of his backpack for the fourth or fifth time that day.

"I fell into a crack," Henry told them haltingly. "Scotty went for help."

"Was Scotty injured?" Helma asked.

Henry shook his head. "He's fine," he said, closing his eyes again.

"Here, Helma," Ruth said from her top bunk as they were preparing for their second and last night in the emergency cabin. "There's an article in this art magazine you should read."

"No thanks," Helma told her. "Later."

"Read it while you're standing guard tonight," Ruth persisted. "It's about biblio-whatevermacallit. Just take it."

Helma was about to decline the offer a second time when she saw the expression in Ruth's eyes. She stood and reached for the magazine. Ruth raised it, exposing what lay on her bunk next to her side.

It was Ruth's camera. The back was open and the exposed film curled from the canister, unwound, destroying the photos she'd taken of the stranded group.

Helma had first watch that night. She sat at the picnic table with a ration of five M&M's beside her, and related the day's events in her notebook, skipping a line between each significant incident, letting the words "Personal Tensions" stand by themselves to describe the day's multitudinous bickering and heated exchanges. "Henry Lanyon semialert," she noted, glancing over at the injured man who slept so deeply none of their activities in the cabin even made him flinch. For the destroyed film, she wrote, "Film overexposed," underlining the word "overexposed." Whoever had opened Ruth's camera wanted to be sure there was no photographic record of their presence. Why bother, when there were six witnesses?

She shivered; at least for the moment there were six witnesses.

The cabin was quiet but Helma doubted if anyone except Henry was asleep, rather that they'd chosen once again to withdraw from one another, going to bed early to hasten the arrival of morning and their departure from the emergency cabin and each other's company.

She shoved two more pieces of wood into the stove, watching the coals spark and leap to life, red flames lapping along the sides of the fresh logs. Fire was mesmerizing.

She remembered the summer night in her parents' backyard when her cousin Ricky had set fire to her tent, how her first reaction had been amazement, not terror, at the blooming flames. Not until her father had emerged roaring from the house and pulled her from her disintegrating tent did the enormity of the event hit her. She'd lain calmly in her father's arms while her mother called the fire department, the police, and a priest, and her cousin Ricky raced across the yard and away in his bare feet, hiding in Aunt Em's barn and eating raw chicken eggs for three days.

Outside, the dark and snowy night pressed around the little cabin, snow shifted on trees or slid off the roof or just piled itself deeper and deeper.

Brentley tossed on his bunk, twisting and turning inside his sleeping bag. And Judith lay so still, Helma was positive the older woman was awake, listening to every movement.

Helma was restless herself, unable to settle her thoughts, aware of the uneasy thudding of her heart. She'd never appreciated close quarters or tight fits, preferring room to stretch, and spaces with entrances and exits to the wider world plainly marked. Nor did she appreciate games involving disappearing guns, missing batteries, and exposed film.

The contents of Henry's pockets lay inside an old tuna can that still held the waxy remains of a white candle. She idly removed one object at a time: his diabetic card, twine, change, Swiss army knife, broken sunglasses, and the key ring holding two keys. First she lined the items in a row perpendicular to a crack in the picnic table, then following the crack, and finally in a circle. That didn't occupy much time.

As BonBon sneezed twice, followed immediately by a husky "Bless you" from Judith, Helma picked up the key chain holding the medallion and two keys. One appeared the size and shape of a suitcase key, the other similar to a car key. Helma held the medallion close to the lamp. Ruth had stated with authority that in real life Henry was an accountant because he carried a CPA medallion like a good luck charm.

The medallion didn't read CPA, meaning certified public accountant; it read SPA. Helma held the medal close to the camp light and studied the little bronze disk, turning it front to back.

Seattle Pilots' Association, the raised writing on the verso read, above a tiny embossed airplane. She should have examined the key chain herself instead of trusting it to Ruth's exuberant conclusion-jumping.

She returned the items to the tuna can, wondering if Henry owned his own plane. At that moment he stirred, groaning a little. Helma carried a fresh glass of water to his bunkside, where he struggled to sit up, then collapsed back on the bunk.

"No thanks," he whispered. "It only makes me need to . . . you know."

Seeing to Henry's personal needs had taken subtle maneuvering, done by Whittaker with clinical matter-of-factness. Whittaker was so effective, Helma decided, precisely because he didn't care about any of them.

"You belong to the Seattle Pilots' Association," Helma said. "I saw your key chain medallion."

He nodded and felt his growth of beard with his good hand, as if he'd just discovered its presence.

"Do you have a plane?"

"No more," he said, his voice raspy and dry. "Too expensive."

"But you still fly?"

"Sometimes." He gripped Helma's hand, his dark eyes rimmed with red. "The way you talked . . . What happened to Scotty? Is he dead?"

There was no sense lying. "He is," Helma told him. "I'm sorry."

Henry took a deep breath and released Helma's hand, seeming to sink into his sleeping bag. "Will we leave soon?" he asked. "I need . . ."

"In the morning," Helma assured him. "Everything's set. By tomorrow afternoon you'll be safe in the hospital and on your way to a complete recovery, I promise you."

He nodded, then closed his eyes and Helma rose, seeing as she turned a glint of lantern light reflecting from BonBon's open eyes.

chapter fifteen

DISAPPEARANCE

"Wake up, Helma. We have a problem."

Into Helma's rousing mind appeared an image of the Apollo 13 crew: *Houston, we have a problem.*

She sat up, astronauts receding, immediately alert, opening her eyes to Ruth's frowning countenance.

"What is our problem?" Helma asked as she straightened the edges of her sleeping bag and glanced at her watch: it was six-thirty; she'd overslept.

"Whittaker and BonBon are gone."

Helma pulled aside her emergency blanket curtain and made a visual sweep of the cabin. The lanterns were lit. Judith and Brentley stood beside the stove, Brentley's face dark with irritation, Judith's drawn in worry. Henry Lanyon lay in his bunk, eyes open but his expression distant, removed from the unfolding drama. Whittaker's bunk was empty, as if he'd never sulked within its confines. Not a trace of his presence remained. "He took the radio with him," Helma commented.

"Well, there goes today's entertainment," Ruth said.

"I'll be out in a moment," Helma said, dropping the space blanket and hurriedly pulling on her clothes. She rose from her bunk and folded her sleeping bag before examining the rest of the cabin.

A pink and green scarf lay on BonBon's upper bunk like a discarded memento, but her backpack and jacket were gone. Her deluxe first-aid kit still sat on the floor beside Henry's sick bed. "She left this," Helma said, picking up the plastic kit.

"Leaving the cabin was very dangerous," Judith said, her husky voice strained. "We've had too many variations in snow and wind and temperatures in the past several hours. It turned colder last night and light snow has piled on top of heavy snow." Her voice ran on in frantic concern. "When the temperatures rise, it could be a disaster. The slopes are unstable and for someone unfamiliar with the mechanics of avalanches . . ."

Brentley patted Judith's shoulder and Judith looked at him beseechingly. "In 1910, after several days of snow," she told him, "avalanches swept two trains off the mountain near Wellington, south of us. Ninety-six people died.

"Look out there," she said in a distraught voice, pointing out the window toward the white world. "And now those two young people . . ."

"Whittaker strikes me as being experienced," Brentley assured Judith with unusual generosity. "He'll be careful."

"When did you discover Whittaker and BonBon were gone?" Helma asked.

"About forty-five seconds before I woke you up," Ruth told her.

Henry focused on Helma and asked, "Who's gone?"

"Two of our companions," Helma told him. "But that doesn't change our plans."

"Blond," Henry had said during his fever, almost as a warning. And now both blonds were gone. She wasn't as surprised by Whittaker's disappearance as she was by

BonBon's. She'd anticipated Whittaker's bolting from the first few moments of his arrival.

"At least Whittaker waited until Henry's fever broke before he left," Helma said to Ruth.

"Unless Whittaker was the one who *caused* his fever," Ruth responded. "Remember his vile-smelling magic potion? Maybe it didn't work the way he'd planned so he skipped out before the authorities showed up."

Helma idly turned the first-aid kit as she thought, examining the elaborate box. "This is curious," she said.

"What's that?" Ruth asked.

"The price tag is still on this first-aid kit."

"Yeah, you'd expect the very first thing BonBon would do would be to strip off all her price tags."

"She bought the kit at the Sports Corral in Bellehaven," Helma said.

"So?"

"So she said she drove up to the trailhead from Seattle."

Ruth shrugged. "Maybe she stopped in Bellehaven first. Considerate of her to leave it here. We may need it."

Helma set the kit back on the floor and moved to the window beside the door. The morning was lighter, the snowflakes fewer and drifting lazily rather than being driven by winds. The storm was either finally abating or this was another pause in its intensity. A softened landscape of white stretched in every direction, the trees in the stand beside the cabin a huddle of humpy white and green.

"They must have left several hours ago," she mused out loud.

"How do you know?" Brentley asked.

"Any tracks leading away from the cabin have been filled in by snow," Helma told him. "Obliterated."

"Elementary, my dear Utterson," Ruth added.

"And no one heard or saw them leave?" Helma asked, looking at Judith, who'd claimed to be such a light sleeper.

"Obviously they left during one of their own watches," Brentley said. "Whittaker and BonBon had the last two watches before morning. That would have given them a good four hours' start, easy."

"In the dark?" Ruth asked.

As one, she and Helma looked up at the shelf where the flashlights had been lined up beside the store of food. Only one remained, Brentley's krypton light.

Once again, Helma peered out at the stunted and laden trees, the smooth snow. "The wind's dropped," she said. "Traveling might be easier."

"The rats went alone," Ruth commented. "That's too rude. To leave us here with a sick man. It would serve them right if . . ."

"Don't say it," Judith warned, her eyes steely and voice firm. "No one deserves bad luck on the mountain."

"Sorry," Ruth mumbled. "So now what do we do? The weather's improved. Do we sit tight and wait to be rescued? I suppose my underwear still bravely waves o'er our ramparts."

"Henry does seem better, quieter. His fever *has* broken," Judith pointed out. "It might be safer to wait for assistance, even if he does need insulin."

"This may only be a break in the storm," Helma reminded them.

"But if Whittaker and BonBon are out there, say stuck in a snowbank," Ruth suggested, "we might stumble across them on our way down."

It was a dilemma. From the time Helma was a little girl, she'd been told, "If you're lost, stay put." But there was Henry, with his injuries and his need for insulin:

would waiting increase his chances of dying or would moving him increase his chances of complications, or death as well? And if this was only a break in bad weather . . . BonBon and Whittaker might already have met rescuers who were searching for them. Or the couple could be lost, or even swept away by one of Judith's avalanches.

But why had the couple left so secretively? *Sneaking* away?

Judith's distracted expression cleared. "I remember where I've seen Whittaker before," she said. "At the university hospital in Seattle."

"He *is* a doctor," Ruth said. "I knew it."

Judith frowned and shook her head. "No, not a doctor, but when I saw him he was *with* a doctor making his rounds. My impression was that he was a student."

"When did you see him?" Helma asked.

"About a year ago. He's a memorable person." She sighed. "So handsome."

"Not much of a bedside manner, though," Ruth commented. "Not even his looks can make up for that."

When Judith and Brentley became involved in an urgent and low conversation on the edge of Judith's bunk, Ruth stood beside Helma, who was rolling her sleeping bag into a tight roll, turning a sliver of firewood between her fingers like a miniature baton. "You know," she said softly. "BonBon and Whittaker didn't strike me as a crazy-in-love couple about to run off together."

"What do you mean?" Helma asked.

"I'm more experienced in these matters than you are, Helm, so trust me. I'd swear Whittaker was not, I repeat *not*, interested in our pink cupcake. I'd bet a pair of snowshoes and a hot buttered rum that he didn't invite her for a stroll in the snow."

"Do you think she followed him?"

Ruth tossed the twirling sliver in the air and easily

caught it. ''That's exactly what I think. Whittaker had things to hide, believe me. Remember the size of his pack? It was like he was on safari, not just a little hike in the hills. There's something funny about that guy. He bolted for the great outdoors on his own rather than suffer our congeniality—or a chance he'd meet up with a bunch of authority figures. BonBon couldn't accept she wasn't drop-dead attractive to any man and went after him, expecting he'd tuck her beneath his sizable biceps and usher her off the mountain so she could keep her manicure and frosting appointment at Chez Hair.''

''But he wouldn't have left her to flounder in the snow by herself,'' Helma protested.

Ruth shrugged. ''She'd just slow him down. Compassion didn't exactly ooze from his pores.''

''Maybe not on a personal level but he took care of Henry—attentively—despite protesting he didn't intend to become involved.''

''Henry was a scientific experiment to Whittaker, a puzzle, not a personal encounter.'' Ruth sighed. ''We already know Whittaker's immune to the charms of beautiful women,'' she said, pointing her stick baton at herself.

Helma paused, one knee resting atop her tightly rolled sleeping bag. ''I think we know where the gun is now, too.''

''Jesus H.,'' Ruth said. ''The gun.'' She shuddered. ''So not only could BonBon be lost between here and the snow line, she could also be . . .'' and Ruth made her hand into a gun shape, jerking it like a shot.

''Possibly,'' Helma agreed, tying the loops around her sleeping bag. There was no time to waste.

''Did you know BonBon's hobby is entomology?'' Helma asked as she fastened her sleeping bag to her pack.

''Ent or Et?''

"Ent: insects."

"Weird."

Helma nodded. "Unusual," she agreed, thinking of BonBon's watchful eyes beneath her delicately shaped brows.

"Since you've appointed yourself head of this expedition, Helma," Brentley interrupted, "what do you recommend we do now?"

Helma had quickly sorted through the avenues open to them and made a choice. "Ruth and I will go down the mountain," Helma said, ignoring Ruth's squawk. "We'll send help immediately. You and Judith remain here with Henry."

"That won't work," Brentley said, vigorously shaking his head. "I'm going. I have to."

"Yeah," Ruth agreed. "Let him go. He's all hot to get out of here for some reason." She pointed her stick at him. "And it ain't a meeting."

"You don't know anything about me," he said.

"I know enough," Ruth told him smugly.

"Transporting Henry would be difficult when the trail's been obliterated and we don't know how far the snow extends," Helma explained to Brentley. "Without Whittaker and BonBon's help, we don't have any margin for error. At the same time, we don't know Whittaker and BonBon's situation. If only Ruth and I go, Henry's safe and we increase our chances of being rescued."

"That's what you say," Brentley argued, pacing between the stove and Judith's bunk. His face was red, his mouth pursed, the hairpiece above his forehead misaligned. His soft body was tense.

"Calm down," Ruth said. "Have a drink; there's still some whiskey in the bottle at the foot of my bunk. Or go smoke a cigarette."

"He gave them up," Judith told them, smiling at Brentley. "Isn't that wonderful?"

"But I smelled cigarette smoke on you yesterday," Helma said.

"It was his last one," Judith supplied. "He only brought two with him."

"Two packs?" Ruth asked.

"Two cigarettes," Brentley told her morosely. "I was trying to quit."

Suddenly Helma understood. "How many cigarettes were you smoking a day?" she asked Brentley.

"A pack and a half."

"And you only brought two cigarettes for a week-long hike?"

"I thought if I was up here and couldn't get any more, I'd have to quit cold turkey. That was the plan anyway."

"Hold on," Ruth said. "That's why you're a nervous wreck? Because you're going through nicotine withdrawal?"

"And you're anxious to get off the mountain to buy cigarettes, not because of a meeting," Helma guessed.

Judith stared at Brentley, shaking her head once as if she couldn't believe what she heard. "You want to buy *cigarettes?*"

"So what?" he asked. "When I get down, I'll go see my doctor and get a nicotine patch. I'll still quit."

"Cigarettes," Judith said to herself. "He wanted to buy cigarettes, no emergency meeting."

"So you're not a bad guy?" Ruth asked. "I mean, comparatively."

"Compared to who?" Brentley asked, frowning.

"Whoever took . . ."

"Ruth," Helma warned, still not ready to trust that Brentley's behavior was due to tobacco withdrawal.

"Okay, so when do we hit the slopes?" Ruth asked in resignation.

"As soon as we're ready. Judith, explain to us again how we can avoid avalanches."

Judith was suddenly alert and purposeful, her eyes lit by the thrill of evasion. "The safest route is along a ridge but stay off the leeward slopes and keep away from cornices," she told them with the authority of a prize-winning teacher. "No narrow ravines, and if you have to rest, stop for as little time as possible. If you're forced to travel across a steep slope, the safest way is to trek diagonally, from top toward the bottom, *not* horizontally. And of course you'll stay off the glacier, not because of avalanches, but hidden crevasses."

They listened attentively, Helma wishing she could take notes that would be readable along their route, and Ruth nodding with glazed eyes.

Helma was prepared for the trek down the mountain, dressed in layers, only the essentials in her pack. As she returned from the amenities, one hand to the rope Brentley had strung and she'd retied, the other holding her scarf over her nose and mouth, she had a better view of their surroundings in the reduced snow and wind.

The snow was powder over heavy wet snow and the new snow fell away from her legs, glittering in the wan light.

For the first time, she saw the cabin clearly: the way it seemed to grow from the slope, the wind and snow-twisted forest close in, crowding to one side and continuing northward up the incline before the terrain opened up to treeless vistas again. Every square inch of land was covered by white, relieved only by the brown cabin walls and the green tree boughs that had shed their snow. She peered upward at the flagpole where Ruth's red underwear—now bedraggled—still did bravely wave. Any searching helicopter crew was sure to see the speck of red against all the white.

She didn't bother pondering whether her decision to leave the cabin was the most reasonable conclusion. At a young age, Helma had learned that when choices were sorted out and found to have equal advantages and disadvantages, the final decision was immaterial. "It doesn't matter what the decision is, Billie," her father had said to her once. "What matters is that you *make* it."

Nearly to the door, Helma let loose of the rope and reached a hand toward the door handle, when her eye was caught by a flash of pink. Low, near the corner of the cabin. Unnatural pink in the white world. She squinted. It was the fingers of a pink glove.

Her heart pounding, Helma approached the glove. It hung like a disembodied hand, caught on a nail on the cabin wall, snow dusted, empty. She plucked it from the wall, then peered further down the snow that sloped away from the cabin, searching for another sign of pink. How could BonBon have gone through the frigid winter landscape wearing only one glove? Why hadn't she turned back?

But the landscape scooped cleanly away, not even the broken sign of passage, the slope of white finally fading to invisibility in the cumulation of lightly falling flakes. Helma raised her hand to her brow, searching for a suspicious bulk covered by white, but saw nothing unusual, only a desolate winter scene, devoid even of birds.

In snow that reached her hips, like pushing through deep water, Helma rounded the corner of the cabin, planning to search in the opposite direction, stopping abruptly, her hopes sinking.

Because in front of her, near the base of the cabin wall, lay a mound of white, the snow uneven and ruffled by recent disturbance. She stood before it, her heart heavy. All she had to do was lean forward and brush away the snow and she'd discover what lay beneath the hump.

Helma briefly considered going back inside the cabin

for help, then decided against it. "It's better if I do this by myself," she said aloud, sadly.

Helma gasped and stumbled backward because, immediately, while her words were frigidly dying on her lips, a pink glove in the shape of a fist was thrust upward through the snow, scattering the light powder into a crystalline cloud.

chapter sixteen

BUTTON, BUTTON . . .

Bracing herself against the cabin wall, adrenaline flowing with fatal urgency, Helma reached forward and grabbed the pink-gloved hand emerging from the snow with both her own, pulling with all her strength.

Had BonBon collapsed in confusion during her vain attempt to leave the cabin during snow and darkness? Judith had claimed that the cries of victims buried beneath snow couldn't be heard while, cruelly, the victim easily heard the efforts of the searchers above. Was this BonBon's last weak attempt to save herself from approaching death?

As Helma tugged, a muffled squeal emitted from the snow, accompanied by BonBon rising from the mound like a mythical being from the sea, snow cascading from her body like water, her blue eyes flashing and her face rosy with cold.

"He keeps making me clear the air passage," she told Helma indignantly, without preamble. "Why can't he do it himself? I'm not his slave. I've had enough. I'm going back inside."

And BonBon pulled herself out of the snow mound

with as much ungainly dignity as possible. She swiped her pink glove from Helma and dragged her backpack behind her in quick angry jerks through the deep snow. "You can have him if you want him," she called back to Helma.

Helma leaned down and peered through the opening made in the mound of snow by BonBon's exit and discovered a small and gloomily lit chamber.

It was a snow cave built against the side of the cabin. No wonder they hadn't spotted it earlier. Not only was it out of sight of the cabin window and the trail to the amenities but it was perfectly camouflaged, white on white. Inside the cave, Whittaker sat curled, his pale eyes gleaming in the light.

"Cozy in there?" Helma asked.

"I didn't invite her to join me," he told Helma. "All I want is a little peace and quiet. You're all driving me crazy."

"If you didn't invite her, why was she here?" Helma asked.

"Ask her."

"Was she searching for something?"

"Beats me," Whittaker said, but he glanced toward his backpack, which lay beside his leg.

"We thought you and BonBon had left the cabin together during the night," Helma said and Whittaker snorted, jerking his head. "Then we worried you might be lost in the snow," Helma told him. "But now we know neither is true, so will you come out of there and help us carry Henry down the mountain? The storm's abated, at least momentarily."

"There's no reason to," Whittaker said sulkily.

"Your strength could make the difference between life and death."

"That's not what I meant."

"Then what do you mean?" Helma asked.

"You figure it out."

"I'm sorry, but I don't play guessing games," Helma told him. "I know about your duties at the university hospital in Seattle," she tried. "What ended your medical training?"

Helma suspected Whittaker was so surprised by her question that he answered without thinking. "I was asked to leave," he said, his voice so raw and pained she knew his dismissal had been recent.

"And so you retired to the mountains to cope with the disappointment?"

"I'd appreciate it if you'd leave me alone," he said, his voice once again guarded and flat.

"This is absurd," Helma told him, her temper rising as she stood in hip-deep snow, bending over and speaking through a hole to a man huddled inside a pile of snow. "We're in a dangerous situation together and you're behaving like the spoiled child whose afternoon has been ruined by the grownups. You don't want to be bothered by us but then you disappear and cause *us* worry. Where's the independence in that?"

"I didn't ask to join this bunch of maniacs."

Helma pulled back from his hole in the snow, saying wearily, "Yes, I know, and you didn't ask to be born, either, right? If this silly little cave had a door, I'd slam it for you, and happily leave you to wait out the weather until spring."

"No need," Whittaker snapped and Helma found herself looking at the frame of his backpack which he'd shoved against the opening of his snow cave.

Let him freeze, Helma thought, as she brushed the snow from her clothing as best she could and returned to the cabin. BonBon sat at the picnic table, tearfully relating her woeful tale to Judith, while seated across from them, Ruth rolled her eyes in exaggeration.

"He doesn't care whether we live or die," BonBon

told Judith as she wiped her eyes with the sleeve of her jacket.

"You mean he doesn't care whether *you* live or die," Ruth amended. "Blow to the ego, right?"

"Ruth," Helma warned and removed a clean tissue from her left pocket and gave it to BonBon. "What did Whittaker have that you wanted?" she asked.

BonBon pulled the tissue away from her pink nose. "What do you mean?"

Ruth rubbed her hands together gleefully and leaned closer across the table, head turning between Helma and BonBon.

"You were searching for an item in his backpack," Helma guessed.

"The radio," BonBon said, dabbing at her nose. "Didn't you want it?"

"Then why didn't you just ask him for it?"

BonBon sniffed and pushed back a lock of hair with a manicured but chipped nail. "He's so mean he wouldn't have given it to me if I'd asked politely like any normal person."

"So where is it?" Ruth asked.

"Where's what?" BonBon returned.

"The r-a-d-i-o," Ruth spelled out.

"Oh. I couldn't find it." BonBon shoved the tissue in her pocket, then stood and lugged her pink backpack to her bunk. End of conversation.

Henry lay propped on his bunk, sleeping bag pulled to his shoulders, watching the women with mild interest. Brentley took BonBon's seat beside Judith at the picnic table.

"That's a handsome backpack," Helma said, following behind BonBon.

"Thank you."

"Did you buy it at the Sports Corral, too?"

"They were having a sale . . ." BonBon stopped with

one foot on the end of Judith's bed to hoist herself to the top bunk. She turned and gave Helma a quizzical, considering glance.

"I saw the label on the first-aid kit," Helma said.

"Oh." BonBon lowered herself back to the floor. She sat on the edge of Judith's bunk, smoothing Judith's sleeping bag behind her as if she were worried about wrinkles. "So now you're curious why I bought my equipment in Bellehaven when I'm from Seattle, right?"

"Frankly, yes," Helma told her.

BonBon sighed and picked at her chipped fingernail. "The people I was supposed to meet for this hike? Person, really; he's my boyfriend. He lives in Bellehaven and we see each other every week. Either I drive up to visit him or he comes down to Seattle to see me. We planned this trip a month ago and he helped me pick out the equipment at the Sports Corral then, that's all."

"But then he stood you up," Ruth said. "Left you standing at the trailhead? Right?"

They were interrupted by Whittaker banging open the cabin door and stomping into the cabin without a word and without a glance toward any of the cabin's inhabitants. With the maximum amount of noise, he dropped his pack on his bunk and moved to the stove to stand before it warming his hands, his big body filling the small space. He might as well have been alone in the cabin. BonBon gave him a bitter look and then went on as if he hadn't interrupted the conversation at all.

"I *wasn't* stood up,' " she told Ruth. "I've *never* been stood up in my life, ever. We had a fight and our hiking plans were left up in the air. I waited at the trailhead for two hours, I gave him every chance. And then Brentley came along so I hiked with him. I didn't see any sense in wasting my equipment."

"But earlier you said the clerk helped you choose your first-aid kit," Helma reminded her.

"I went back for the first-aid kit by myself," BonBon said. "It seemed smart to carry one."

"How about carrying a gun?" Ruth asked.

"Of course not," BonBon said, not appearing at all surprised by the question.

But at the picnic table, Judith Poole shifted uncomfortably and stood, her mouth forming an o, which Helma wouldn't have noticed if Brentley hadn't called attention to the two of them by joining Judith and saying, "Forget about that gun."

"*That* gun?" Helma asked, turning to face Brentley. "Exactly which gun are you talking about?"

Judith bit her lip. "Oh, I didn't want to bring it up," she told Helma.

Brentley placed a comforting hand on Judith's shoulder and said, "She's talking about *your* gun."

Judith nodded and looked sadly at Helma. "I was surprised to see you hiding a pistol in your backpack that first night. You didn't seem at all like the kind of woman to carry a *gun*. I mean, you being a librarian and everything."

"It wasn't my gun," Helma said. "I found it in . . ."

"You *found* a gun?" Judith interrupted, gazing at Helma in reproachful disbelief.

BonBon's eyes narrowed. "*You* had the gun?" she asked Helma.

Brentley raised his eyebrows. "A librarian with a gun. What's this world coming to?"

"She just hates it when people mess up books on the shelves," Ruth said.

"Bloody hell," Whittaker muttered from beside the stove, looking as if he wanted to jam his fingers into his ears.

"I *wasn't* carrying a gun," Helma tried to clarify again, noting how everyone had moved closer to her, gathering around her. "I found it in the bottom of my sleeping bag."

"Right," Brentley said. "And how did it get *there*?"

"Wait a minute," Ruth said, raising her hands and halting the conversation. "Let's get this straight." She pointed to Helma. "Miss Wilhelmina Zukas here, found a gun in her sleeping bag. Imagine her surprise and wonder. Now *that* was a little gift she hadn't expected. So instead of asking if any of us had misplaced a semiautomatic pistol—that's what it was, a semiautomatic, right Helma?—she shoved the gun in her backpack for safekeeping."

"I would have asked who lost it," BonBon said.

"Hold on," Ruth told BonBon. "The gun disappeared because Judith saw Helma put it in her backpack and then, Judith, you took the gun from Helma's backpack?"

Judith nodded. "During the night. I didn't know why she had a gun but it certainly isn't wholesome to carry firearms. In my experience, common sense is a better protection against wild animals than a gun. I told her that myself." She looked at Helma sternly and said, "Guns simply aren't necessary up here."

"Then what did *you* do with the gun?" Ruth asked Judith.

Judith gazed up at Brentley. "I gave it to Brentley. I'm not comfortable with firearms."

BonBon pointed to Brentley. "And *you* gave the gun to Whittaker."

Brentley shook his head. "Hardly. I wouldn't purposely place a weapon in that man's hands. I don't trust his type. Strong and silent, people say, well, that's only on the surface. Still waters run deep. But rest assured the gun's in a very safe place."

"Well, who in hell stashed the damn thing in Helma's sleeping bag in the first place?" Ruth demanded. "And why? And was it loaded?"

"It was heavy," Helma told her. "The magazine may have held bullets."

Judith shrugged and Brentley said, "I didn't check the magazine."

Whittaker shoved a log in the woodstove and slammed the cast-iron door. "Will you all just shut up? Yes. The gun *is* loaded. *I* found the gun and *I* put it in Helma's sleeping bag." He gave Helma a glance of disappointment. "I expected you to be more responsible with it."

"Then you might have included written instructions," Helma told him.

"I didn't want to get involved," Whittaker said.

"You could hardly avoid that," Helma told him. "But where did *you* find the gun?"

Whittaker turned and looked at Henry lying in his bunk. "It was in his pants pocket. I found it when I changed his clothes."

Brentley said, "Oh Lord" so loud they all turned to stare at his dismayed countenance.

Helma was the first to realize the implications and took two hurried steps toward Henry's bunk but BonBon, in one swift lunge, was there ahead of her.

"Beneath the bag," Henry said. "Under my left thigh."

"Get back, all of you," BonBon said, reaching beneath Henry's sleeping bag and extricating the gun. She handled the little pistol with familiarity and Helma found herself crazily wondering if BonBon shot insects out of the air for sport. "By the stove," BonBon ordered. "Everyone."

"Clever move," Ruth told Brentley. "You put the gun right back where it started. Congratulations."

"How was I supposed to know?" Brentley asked peevishly. "If the Nordic god here had told us he'd found a gun in the first place instead of playing musical pistols with it, this wouldn't be happening."

"By the stove, I said," BonBon repeated. "Raise your hands."

"Oh come on," Ruth said. "That makes me feel so stupid. You're the only one here with a weapon."

"Do it," she ordered, and they did, backing toward the woodstove.

Henry laboriously raised himself to a sitting position in his bunk. He was weak, his face ashen. If only he'd been the one with the gun, Helma thought, they'd have a better chance than with the cool-eyed BonBon, who stood patiently waiting for them all to gather in a tight knot beside the stove.

"Good job, honey," Henry said.

"Honey," Ruth repeated. "I guess that means you two have met before today, huh?"

"Don't bother trying to figure it out," BonBon said.

"Okay," Ruth said amiably.

"I'm guessing that isn't Henry Lanyon," Helma said. "But you were wearing his clothes, weren't you? That's why you have severe blisters; his hiking boots didn't fit."

"He doesn't have diabetes, either," Whittaker said. "It didn't take long to figure that out."

"For somebody in the know, anyway," Brentley snarled at Whittaker. "Another small detail you might have shared with us."

"But Henry *did* have diabetes." Helma looked at the ashen man and softly asked, "Where's the real Henry?"

He didn't even blink and Helma felt a wave of sad certainty that Scotty's partner, the real Henry Lanyon, was dead, too. That's how the imposter had obtained the hiking clothes; he'd killed Henry and taken them. She glanced at the gun in BonBon's hand, wondering if it had been the instrument to end both Scotty and Henry's lives.

Henry bumped, Bradshaw had reported Scotty saying.

Not bumped, but bumped off: murdered. If only Scotty had said "killed." It was one more proof of the need for accuracy in the English language.

"My keys?" the pseudo-Henry said to BonBon.

BonBon pulled the chain holding the Seattle Pilots' Association medallion and the two keys from her pants pocket. "Right here. Where did you leave it?" she asked him.

"I know exactly where it is."

"You can't keep one gun trained on all of us for very long," Helma said reasonably. She stood in front of Ruth and Whittaker, the tallest, realizing they'd arranged themselves like a class photo, tallest in the rear.

"We'll be leaving soon," BonBon said.

"Who's the strongest?" the injured man asked BonBon.

"Those two," BonBon told him, pointing over Helma's head to Ruth and Whittaker.

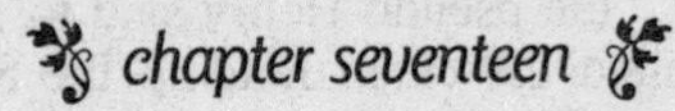

chapter seventeen

HITTING THE TRAIL

"I don't get it," Ruth told BonBon
"What's being strong got to do with having a gun hel
to our heads? Are you planning on forced calisthenics?'
BonBon calmly turned the gun toward Ruth, pointin
the barrel directly between Ruth's eyes. "I'm so tired o
your mouth. Do you know what would give me grea
pleasure?"

Ruth held her hands higher. "You want pushups? Jus
tell me how many."

Helma took a single swift step in front of Ruth, al
though BonBon's gun was aimed six inches abov
Helma's head. "What Ruth means," she said to BonBo
in a conversational tone, even attempting to add a touc
of earnestness, "is that we're all willing to cooperat
with you. Exactly what would you like us to do?"

"Get the litter ready," BonBon told her, nodding t
the folded blue tarp. "Put all the sleeping bags togethe
and we'll need two backpacks. Plus the first-aid kit—th
one *I* brought."

"If you're planning on our transporting Henry—o
whatever his actual name is—down the mountain, w
already have an efficient plan drafted for that."

"You three," BonBon waved the gun toward Helma, Judith, and Brentley, "will be staying here."

"Oh," Ruth said. "That's why you're looking for the strongest. Am I correct in assuming Whittaker and I will be carrying your little wounded buddy down the mountain?"

"Not *down* the mountain," Helma corrected, keeping her eyes on BonBon and her gun. "You'd hardly need a gun to encourage us to hike *down* the mountain into the arms of weapon-carrying law enforcement teams who are at this very moment making their way toward this cabin, intent on rescuing us."

"They are?" Ruth asked.

"Perhaps even reporters looking for a story of dramatic rescue," Helma continued. "The law and reporters are the last people this couple cares to meet. I'm guessing our friends plan to take another course. North, *across* the mountains, am I right?"

Judith gasped and Helma continued, "No, your destination is *out* of the United States of America, and here we are, conveniently only two miles from the Canadian border. And from Canada, where? To the tropical beaches he feverishly hallucinated about?"

Judith Poole stepped forward, her hands open, and said to BonBon, "Now that the snows have begun, it's insane to attempt to reach Canada through the mountains. During the summer, following Edward Ridge to the Canadian border is a fairly strenuous hike, but it's been snowing and blowing for forty-eight hours. The trail is completely buried and the snow is unstable. I've hiked that route in good weather and I *know* what the ridge is like. The slope is generally thirty to forty degrees, perfect for a deadly avalanche."

"The border's less than two miles from here," BonBon said patiently. "It's a mostly level walk, in fact, according to Helma's detailed maps"—here she inclined her head in gratitude toward Helma—"the ridge slopes downhill. It shouldn't take more than three hours, tops."

Judith blew an exasperated sigh, her lower lip out and fluttering the short fringe of hair across her forehead.

"What crime have you committed," Helma asked, "that you'd risk your lives like this? You probably stand a better chance dealing with the law."

"Tall doesn't naturally signify strong," Ruth said, still deliberating over the subject of strength. "You think I'm stronger than he is?" She pointed to Brentley, who stood behind Judith, one hand on her shoulder.

Instead of pulling in and straightening his body as Helma expected, Brentley shriveled before their eyes: his head thrust forward as if it were too heavy for his neck, his shoulders sagged and his stomach pooched out. Even the freckles on his reddish skin managed to look like age spots.

"Never mind," Ruth amended. She looked from Judith to Helma, appraising, then shook her head. "I guess I'm your woman."

"Once you reach the Canadian border—if you do," Helma said, "you still have to work your way out of the mountains. The snow doesn't stop at the border. This will be far more than a three-hour jaunt."

"Then I hope your friends are in good shape."

Suddenly Whittaker roughly pushed Helma aside and with one long muscular stride, was at the injured man's bunk. Before BonBon could move he'd placed his hands around "Henry's" throat. Henry's pale face began to redden as Whittaker purposefully squeezed and stared BonBon in the eye. "Drop your gun," he ordered her. "I can snap his neck before a bullet hits me."

For the briefest moment, Helma believed BonBon would obey Whittaker's command. Her mouth worked, the gun wavered, but then she stiffened and stepped up to Brentley, pointing the gun an inch from his temple

"Get away from him or I'll shoot Brentley—dead."

Brentley made a strangled sound deep in his throat; his lips trembled helplessly. Whittaker slightly relaxed his hands around Henry's throat and the man wheezed, gasping for air. Then Whittaker frowned at BonBon and Brentley, tipping his pale and handsome head. He shrugged and retightened his grip around Henry's throat.

"Go ahead," he told BonBon.

"No!" Brentley cried out.

"Damn it," BonBon said, shoving Brentley aside and grabbing Helma by the arm, jamming the barrel of the pistol into Helma's neck. "How about this one?" she asked Whittaker.

It was a standoff. Whittaker and BonBon gazed into each other's eyes, each judging the other's resolve, Whittaker squeezing as Henry weakly struggled, turning red, and BonBon pushing the pistol barrel painfully into Helma's throat.

Helma didn't move; she didn't blink. She smelled BonBon's perfume and felt the cool barrel against her neck and BonBon's rigid grip on her arm. The barrel bore into her throat. Don't panic, she told herself. From somewhere came her Uncle Juozas's voice, teaching her her favorite girlhood poem, "The Gingham Dog and the Calico Cat," in Lithuanian:

Kartūninis katinas ir šuo iš velveto
šalia vienas kito ant stalo susėdo,
Kaip as ir zinojau . . .

And then she was released. Helma swallowed, watching Whittaker—his face blank in defeat—drop his hands and step away from Henry's bunk, rejoining the group while Henry coughed and gasped.

"That was so brave," Judith said, sighing.

"It looks like I found your soft spot," BonBon said

to Whittaker, letting go of Helma but pinching her hard before she did, on her face a scowl of jealous indignation.

"Who'da thunk it?" Ruth murmured from behind Helma.

Under BonBon's steely stare and her accomplice's less steady gaze, the captive group got to work, doing as BonBon bid. She stood beside Henry's bunk, where she could keep an eye on all of them as they complied with her orders.

The homemade litter was lined with two sleeping bags, and two backpacks were filled with food, first-aid supplies, dry clothes, flashlights, and a map, seriously depleting the stores for the three to be left behind. BonBon oversaw their every move, transferring the gun occasionally from her right hand to her left, appearing equally at ease employing either hand.

"Your name must actually be Jennie," Helma said as she refolded a pair of heavy wool socks and tucked them in the corner of the backpack.

"Guess again," BonBon said.

Helma nodded toward the injured man rubbing his throat. "When he was delirious with fever, that's the name he was calling."

"That's right," Ruth agreed from beside the bunks where she was layering on a pair of Judith's pants beneath her skirt, the hems ending at midcalf. "Jennie. He sounded desperate, broken-hearted even, like his beloved Jennie had been ripped from his arms. He must really be crazy about you."

BonBon's forehead creased. She frowned at Ruth and Helma, then at Henry reclining in his bunk. "Jennie," she repeated. "You did call out for Jennie. I thought you were trying to throw them off the track." She hesitated. "Weren't you?"

His pained face grew more pained. If he'd been

healthier he might have been able to think faster, or at least deny what Helma and Ruth implied and BonBon questioned.

"Honey," he said weakly. "You know . . ."

"I know what?" BonBon cut him off, the gun momentarily wavering. "There really *is* a Jennie, isn't there? Who is she?"

"Oh, it's probably just the name he christened his airplane," Ruth suggested in a syrupy soothing voice that barely disguised her delight in BonBon's discomfort. "Like Jenny Lind, the pilot."

"Jenny Lind was a nineteenth-century singer," Helma told Ruth. "Her sobriquet was 'the Swedish Nightingale.' "

"No she wasn't," Ruth argued. "She tried to fly across the ocean and disappeared and was eaten by cannibals."

"You're thinking of Amelia Earhart," Judith broke into the discussion, slipping away from Brentley, who'd kept a low profile since being threatened by BonBon and abandoned by Whittaker. "And there's no evidence of her fate, none at all." Judith's eyes went dreamy. "Not a clue. She simply vanished. Gone forever."

"Just like your plane beneath all this snow," Helma said casually to the man lying on the bunk.

"I know right where . . ." Henry began, but BonBon motioned him quiet, laying a hand on his good shoulder.

"Hot dog," Ruth said. "I think we've hit pay dirt."

"So you crashed your airplane in the mountains in an attempt to fly to Canada where a boat or plane was waiting to transport you somewhere sunny and safe," Helma guessed.

"Who's Jennie?" BonBon asked again.

"Nobody. An old friend."

"What are you running from?" Ruth asked.

"Rudy," BonBon said sternly. "I demand that you explain who Jennie is."

"Rudy," Ruth repeated. "Your name's Rudy, as in Rudolph of red nose fame?"

"With an f, not a ph," the newly unmasked Rudy said from his bed, his weak voice touched by disdain.

"Rudolf," Helma said, frowning, searching her formidable memory. "Wasn't that the name of the vitamin king, the one on the radio who bilked people out of millions?"

"Heaven's Nutrients?" Brentley asked, rising from the backpack he was struggling to close, turning his soft hands into fists. "Why, you . . . I pulled money out of my retirement account for that scheme."

"And lost every penny, I bet," Ruth said.

"Where's your partner?" Helma asked. "The radio said there were two of you. Did he die in the plane crash?"

"Is that ready?" BonBon asked, nodding to the litter.

"Pretty much," Ruth told her. "Care to hop in and try it out?"

BonBon waved the gun menacingly at Ruth. "Finish getting dressed," she ordered. She nodded to Whittaker, who'd grown robotic and distant since his ill-fated attempt to overthrow BonBon. "You, too."

"Your friend Rudy murdered two hikers," Helma told BonBon. "Except Scotty managed to get away. He tried to tell Bradshaw, the man who found him, about an airplane crash, only Bradshaw thought he was referring to the bomber site on Enfield Glacier. He assumed that they'd been hurt trying to reach the bomber, not that they'd discovered a modern air disaster."

Helma studied BonBon and then asked her, "Where were you during all of this? Seattle's south of us but you bought your equipment in Bellehaven, and you didn't buy it a few weeks ago as you claimed, because the

Sports Corral's sale began three days ago. I know because I purchased my equipment too early to take part in it, even though I believe they should have given me a discount in consideration for the amount of money I spent. I *did* buy all my equipment from them."

Helma absently refolded the socks and set them in the opposite corner of the backpack, her mind rolling and unrolling the facts. "No, you were already *in* Bellehaven when your friend attempted his flight to Canada. Did Rudy tell you to wait in Bellehaven for him? Perhaps until he reached Canada and contacted you to join him?"

"Oh, miseries, I know *that* one," Ruth said as she tried to smooth her skirt over the bulky pants she'd pulled on beneath it. "It's as old as the book. The guy promises you he's gonna call and the next thing you know, you're wasting your time sitting beside a silent telephone and he's skipped out with some other woman named Suzie or Sandra, or . . . Jennie."

"But Rudy *did* call you," Helma continued, "when he realized how desperately he needed you. Did he have a cellular phone with him?"

Ruth snapped her fingers. "And Bradshaw said Scotty usually carried a cellular phone."

"I suspect that when Scotty's phone records are traced," Helma continued, "there will be a call to you in a Bellehaven motel, when he asked you to bring the best first-aid kit you could buy and meet him in the mountains for a hike to Canada, or maybe just a hike down to your car and a quick drive across the border. And you were so blindly in love with him, you complied without a second thought."

"You broke the law and risked your life for a guy who's having an affair with some chickie named Jennie," Ruth said, shaking her head.

"That's so sad," Judith Poole agreed. "A pretty girl like you."

"Enough," BonBon ordered, stamping her foot in emphasis. "It's time to go." She stepped back so they all made easier targets. "Help Rudy onto the litter and into a sleeping bag. If there's a screwup, she gets it," and BonBon pointed her gun at Judith.

"Oh my," Judith said huskily, considering BonBon with an even deeper expression of disappointment.

Rudy groaned as they positioned him in the litter. But even as Helma gravely realized that Ruth and Whittaker probably wouldn't be released unharmed even if they did get BonBon and Rudy safely to Canada, she couldn't help but admire the taut efficiency of the hand-fashioned litter. No wonder BonBon had tackled the sewing project so diligently. Rudy was snug and safe, protected by sleeping bags and the securely sewn ends of the tarp. The bear bells jingled as they maneuvered Rudy and the litter.

"The snow's picking up again," Brentley announced, looking out the window.

"We'll leave now," BonBon ordered.

"Wait," Helma said. "Let me check all the seams once before you leave. They'd be easier to fix here."

Whittaker and Ruth were in position, Ruth at the front. From the rear of the litter, Helma studied the two bearers and said, "It makes more sense for Whittaker to be in the front in order to break through the snow. As strong as Ruth is, he has more stamina."

BonBon looked at Helma suspiciously, then ordered Ruth and Whittaker to switch places. Helma tugged at the rear of the litter near Rudy's head in a show of testing the seam, then swiftly untied the lace holding the nylon safety rope she'd attached to guarantee the tarp wouldn't escape again. As Ruth clumped in her heavy clothing to the rear and passed Helma, she thrust the end of the rope into Ruth's gloved hand. "Drop it when you're into the trees," she whispered.

Ruth gripped the rope and said loudly, "When can we get this show on the road? I'm suffocating in all these clothes."

Brentley held open the cabin door and the four trooped outside into the gently falling snow, Whittaker first, holding up his end of the litter; then Ruth at the rear, and finally BonBon, behind Ruth, holding the gun.

The remaining three, Brentley, Judith, and Helma, stood in the doorway regardless of the cold and watched their cabinmates flounder through the deep untracked snow. The litter seemed to cause the least of their problems, the slick cloth skimming through the snow, with Rudy protected by the sleeping bags. The bear bells jingled with each step. Brentley was right; the snow had increased again, the flakes falling in lazy clumps that portended another heavy session.

"What's going to happen to them?" Judith whispered, her hands pressed to her cheeks.

Helma was already turning her green jacket inside out so the paler beige lining faced outward. She had given Ruth her gloves and BonBon had taken her extra pair, so her own hands were bare; there was no helping that.

"An undershirt," she told Brentley. "Give me one of your undershirts. A clean one. Hurry."

"Why?" he asked.

"Just do it," Judith ordered. "Can't you see she has a plan?"

Helma pulled Brentley's undershirt over her hair like a cap and zipped her jacket closed from the inside. "Close the door as soon as I'm through it," she said, "and stay in the cabin."

Whittaker stepped into the stunted trees, bending forward as he broke from a drift into the more sheltered stand where the snow wasn't quite so deep.

Watching their progress, Helma waited until the group was completely into the trees before she slipped through the open door into the clean and featureless white world. Leaving the porch, Helma threw herself to the left, into untrampled snow and hopefully out of BonBon's line of vision.

Snow landed on her face and melted to icy droplets on her warm skin. Her nose ached with the sudden cold and she resisted the urge to pinch her nostrils tight. She'd pulled her hands inside the sleeves of her jacket but already she could feel her fingers stiffening in the frigid air. How could Ruth ever drop the rope without BonBon seeing it?

Helma hid behind the first stunted fir, watching for a sign of the rope trailing through the snow behind Ruth. It was forty feet long, hopefully long enough.

But BonBon walked only a few steps behind Ruth, following in her tracks, too close. Helma emerged from behind one tree and waded through the snow to the next, trying to keep within grabbing distance yet out of sight. She could hear Ruth's voice and tell from its pitch that Ruth was speaking randomly, talking off the top of her head and attempting to keep BonBon distracted. Suddenly, Ruth tripped and the litter slid sideways. BonBon's voice rang out sharply and Ruth scrambled to her feet, still talking. Helma caught the words "Rubens" and "porcine women."

They had fifty feet to go before the trees ended and the landscape changed to the whitely barren and far more dangerous Edward Ridge. There would be no cover on Edward Ridge, only the long sweeping slope of snow, wide open.

But trailing around Ruth's left leg and unfurling behind her was the rope, momentarily out of BonBon's step but Helma knew it would only be a few moments before BonBon caught sight of the line or even stumbled over it.

Keeping low, Helma ran as best she could from behind the trees and perpendicular to the trough made by the litter carriers' passage. The rope lengthened behind Ruth in the dry snow, creating a miniature wake of snowdust.

Ten feet before the trees ended, Helma took a deep breath and threw herself into the snow after the dragging rope. She grabbed its knotted end in her bare hands and twisted, lunging backward, her face full of snow, struggling to reach a substantial dead pine but unable to, then flinging the rope and herself around the trunk of the nearest tree, a small and crooked fir hardly more than a stick. The tree bent under the pressure, the rope slipped, then held, as Helma threw all her weight backward, toppling into the snow on her back, her bare hands gripping the line as if they were already frozen.

She didn't see but heard both Ruth and BonBon's screech, and Rudy's cry, followed immediately by a gunshot. Then the branch from the dead tree next to her crashed down on top of her and Helma's hands released the rope as she slipped gently down into the soft snow.

Certainly she was unconscious. Helma felt herself being carried in the arms of someone large. She smelled a vaguely familiar odor of aftershave and then felt cold lips against her cheek, followed by the whispering of her name.

She opened her eyes to peer into Chief of Police Wayne Gallant's snow-burned cheeks and brilliant blue eyes. He smiled down at her and it was all so delicious she permitted herself to return to unconsciousness at once.

chapter eighteen

RISING BAROMETERS

Helma was first aware of the crowd of people, with all the attendant noises and movements typical of an unorganized throng: laughter, low serious voices, confidential exchanges, milling bodies, the smell of coffee and wet clothing.

"So I guess you paid me back for dragging you across that log on Tower Ford. Even Steven."

It was Ruth, leaning over Helma and holding a cup that smelled alcoholic, although not of Ruth's usual whiskey.

"What are you drinking?" Helma asked.

Ruth guffawed. "This, dear friend, is brandy, brought to us by Bradshaw. Care for a sip?"

"No thanks." Helma sat up and gazed around the emergency cabin. "Bradshaw?" There were too many people. She blinked and tried to count them, giving up at twelve; they just wouldn't stand still. Men in various forms of dress: green uniforms, thermal shirt tops, suspenders, wool shirts. Too big for the small room.

"Maybe a sip," Helma said, taking Ruth's cup and letting the soft liquid slide across her tongue before she swallowed, feeling the warmth spread through her body.

Ruth waved an arm toward the men. "Rescue team," she said, her eyes gleaming appreciatively. "Eight of them scouring the mountains through blizzard and freezing temperatures—think of it—searching for us truly. Refusing to surrender despite life-threatening conditions. Inch by inch up the mountains, never for a moment doubting their mission to . . ."

"I thought I saw . . ." Helma interrupted.

"Oh, you did!" Ruth interrupted in turn. "After your heroic diversion, Whittaker and I wrestled down the BonBon and who should come sweeping out of the snow but . . ." And here, Ruth swept her arms toward the eight rescuers. "While we and the vitamin king were being surrounded by men with big weapons, our valiant chief was scooping you up into his arms and carrying you through the snow to the cabin." Ruth heaved a sigh and patted her heart. "You should have seen it; it would have made a killer cover for a romance novel. *Drifts of Love*."

"Where are BonBon and Rudolf?" Helma asked. She flexed her hands and fingers, which were still stiff from cold.

Ruth nodded toward the corner where Whittaker had bunked. "No tropical paradise for those two."

Pale Rudolf lay on the bunk, his eyes closed while BonBon, her blonde hair damp and flat, slouched on the end of his bunk, her wrists handcuffed to the bunk rail, her face a dark study of anger.

"She's more pissed about Jennie than about being caught," Ruth commented. "And I was right all along: BonBon removed the batteries and pretended to find them again. Exposed the film in my camera, too." Ruth frowned at the left side of Helma's face. "I have some makeup to cover that shiner."

"I believe the term 'shiner' refers to a black eye." Helma gingerly touched her left eye, wincing at the pain, and asked in disbelief, "Are you saying I have a black eye?"

"Not yet. It looks like that tree limb knocked you a hefty smack on the head."

Chief of Police Wayne Gallant separated from the other men near the stove and approached Helma's bunk, a smile on his sun- and wind-burned face, his damp hair pushed back, exposing his widow's peak. He hunkered down beside Helma. "Feeling okay?"

"Almost," Helma told him. "I have a slight headache."

"You were fortunate."

"How did you know where to find us?" Helma asked him.

"We didn't, but knowing you, I figured if you found yourself in bad weather, you'd head for shelter."

"But there are two emergency cabins on this side of the mountain."

He nodded. "Our group split up and luckily I chose to search the right cabin. They found the other missing hikers at the first cabin, not so well equipped as you, but all right."

"You hiked all the way up here?" Helma asked. "Through this weather?"

Wayne Gallant shook his head. "Snowmobiles until it became too dangerous . . . but I would have." The chief stood and stretched his back as if his muscles were stiff. A pair of wide blue suspenders crossed the brown wool shirt he wore over a black turtleneck. Helma hadn't realized before how attractive suspenders were on a man, the way they emphasized his shoulders and chest.

The chief nodded toward the end of Helma's bunk. "Mind if I sit down?"

"Please do," Helma told him. He did and she felt the weight of his hip against her leg. "Is Rudolf the vitamin king?" she asked him.

"That's right. Rudolf Carew. He and his partner flew out of Seattle three days ago. From what we can piece together, they crashed in the mountains. His partner was killed."

"And the man we thought was Henry Lanyon killed the two hikers who tried to help him," Helma finished. "Scotty's puncture wound *was* a bullet hole, wasn't it?"

The chief nodded sadly, saying, "I'm surprised he made it as far as he did."

"Were Rudolf Carew and his business partner attempting to flee to Canada?"

"That's right. That was the first leg of their flight, along with a considerable amount of cash. There's no doubt you saved Rudolf Carew's life," the chief said. "BonBon didn't have the experience to find him."

"But we might have lost Whittaker and Ruth as a consequence," Helma pointed out.

Wayne Gallant, at some point in their conversation, had taken Helma's hand. She hadn't noticed when but she was surprised how quickly her hand warmed in his.

"That's true," he agreed. "You didn't find any cash on Carew?"

"Only a few coins in his pocket, or rather Henry Lanyon's pocket," Helma told him. "He *did* dress in Henry's clothing and hiking books after he killed him, didn't he?"

"It looks that way."

Then Helma remembered the keys. "There was a small key, similar to a suitcase key, attached to his key chain. I know it belonged to Carew, not Henry, because Carew claimed the medallion was his. It was from the Seattle Pilots' Association."

The chief shook his head. "We didn't find any keys."

"I know he took them with him. Did you check inside the sleeping bag? That's where the gun was hidden."

Wayne Gallant stood and went to the jumbled pile of

sleeping bags and the blue tarp that had created Carew's litter. He shook out each piece while BonBon and Carew watched him from Carew's bunk, their faces neutral, but Helma caught the tic at the corner of Carew's mouth.

No keys clattered to the plank floor. Carew leaned back and BonBon's face, without moving, appeared to relax.

"It was a key chain," Helma told Wayne Gallant. "He may have attached it to a zipper pull."

One glance at Carew's frown told Helma she was right and in a few seconds Wayne Gallant triumphantly held up the key chain and keys. He examined the keys and shook his head. "This is the key to his plane and this little one probably fits a briefcase or a suitcase." He regarded BonBon and Carew. "If you left a case full of money in that plane, it may be ten or fifteen years before it's uncovered again."

"Don't forget," Ruth said from the picnic table where Bradshaw—who was as tall standing up as Ruth was sitting—was pouring more brandy into Ruth's aluminum cup, "it was thirty years before enough snow melted off the bomber for it to be found."

"But then," the chief said, "it may be another thirty years before you have the opportunity to search for that plane and whatever it carried."

"Do you know the status of the labor situation at the library?" Helma asked Wayne Gallant. "The radio newscaster said it was being operated by the Friends of the Library."

"That's what I heard."

"But that's like the police department being run by the Boy Scouts," Helma said.

The chief tipped his head to one side. His eyes twinkled. "It might work," he said. Then, seeing Helma's shocked face, he amended, "I'm sure the union has stepped in by now."

"When can we return to Bellehaven?" Helma asked.

"Soon." He squeezed her hand in both of his and Helma forgot everyone else in the cabin. "I'd like us to spend some time together," he told her. "When I saw you lying in the snow . . . Well, we have a lot to talk about."

"Nothing that happened here was as exciting as what happened to *you*," Eve said on Helma's first morning back at the Bellehaven Public Library. "Did you try putting steak on your eye?"

Rain thudded dully against the library's windows; the sky was gray and the mountains behind the city, where the rain, Helma knew firsthand, fell as snow, were invisible.

"Ice," Helma told her. "But the strike? How has it affected our service, the public, our honor?"

Eve shrugged. "You know that new business database we were having trouble with? One of the Friends was a computer whiz. He installed it for us and it works like a champ. And Mrs. Kelly, the Friend who owns the nursery? She replaced all those dying jade plants. But they didn't have time to do much else before the union shut them down. Now *that* made the public mad."

Harley Woodworth, emerging from the staff lounge with a brown bottle of vitamin C tablets in his hand, said, "These are for you. They speed healing." He nodded toward Helma's black eye.

"Thank you but I try to eat properly instead of taking supplements." Harley's face faltered and Helma said, "But you're right; this time I need something stronger than orange juice."

Harley cheerfully opened the bottle for her, unable to shift his eyes from Helma's bruise. "Did the bear bells work?"

"They did," Helma assured him. "We didn't see a single bear."

He nodded sagely. "I knew they would, with that guarantee. You were lucky."

"Very," Helma agreed.

When Helma sorted through the mail that had accumulated during her week away, she came upon Ms. Moon's proclamation that from that day on, the new designation for library employees who were neither librarians nor pages was to be "paraprofessional." And also, paraprofessionals would be permitted to attend library conferences on a rotating basis.

"Welcome back to sea level, Helma," George Melville, the cataloger, said. He pointed to her eye. "That's an attractive shade of green."

Helma held up Ms. Moon's proclamation. "Everyone's satisfied with this settlement?" she asked.

"Ecstatic. Aren't we just a happy little hive of bees?" he asked, sweeping his arms grandly around the workroom where everyone, para and professional alike, was busily attending to library business. "I just saw Ruth Winthrop out front," he continued. "She claims you found romance among the blizzards and criminals. Funny how that's never happened to me."

"You know how Ruth can exaggerate," Helma said. "Is she still in the library?"

"Yup. Look for her in the true adventure section."

Ruth sat on the floor, blocking the aisle that held the high 700's, a stack of books to either side of her. She was dressed in a purple shirt that reached her thighs and tight black pants.

"I thought you were never going to wear pants again," Helma said.

"I've learned my lesson." She held up a book about climbing Mount Everest. "Have you ever read any of these? Our adventure was more exciting than some of this stuff.''

''Are you comparing notes?''

Ruth shook her head. ''I'm looking for ideas. I've decided to write a book about our hiking experience. It'll be called *A Cold Winter's Day*, what do you think?''

''That has a familiar ring,'' Helma said. ''But this is still autumn.''

''Okay, so it'll be *A Cold Autumn's Day*.''

''Ruth,'' Helma said. ''You don't even write letters; what makes you think you can write a book?''

''I can paint, can't I?'' Ruth asked, transferring a book from the stack on her left to the pile on her right. ''All those creative juices come from the same source; you just plug in different tools. Guess who I saw at the police station this morning?''

''I couldn't,'' Helma said, deciding not to inquire why Ruth was at the police station.

''The breathtakingly beautiful Whittaker Newcomen. He was talking to your white knight about police work. Can you imagine him as a cop: 'Sorry, ma'am, I just don't care to get involved.' ''

''He was cool-headed, though,'' Helma reminded her. ''And ultimately, he *did* get involved.''

''Yeah, and he'd be dynamite in a uniform.''

Plus, Helma thought, Whittaker's cool-headedness, instead of being a disadvantage as a doctor, might actually work to his benefit as a policeman.

''Hello,'' a husky voice said from behind Helma.

It was Judith Poole, a wide smile on her face. ''I wanted to see you in your natural environment,'' she said to Helma. ''I didn't expect to see Ruth, too.''

''A reunion,'' Ruth said. ''Is Brentley with you?''

Judith shook her head. ''He's showing me a condo this afternoon, though.''

“And happily smoking by the cartonful?” Ruth asked.

“He says he’ll make an appointment with the doctor to be fitted with one of those nicotine patches,” Judith told her. “Just as soon as he catches up at work.”

“What’ll you do now that there’s too much snow to go back to the mountains?” Helma asked the older woman.

“Oh, I’m on the ski patrol at the ski resort during the season.” She hesitated. “Until then, I thought I’d study some maps of the terrain around Jekyll Glacier. And Helma, the map you put together for your hike was the most detailed I’ve ever seen. Could I, would you mind, if I borrowed it?”

“It’s at home,” Helma told her, “but I’ll make a photocopy of it for you.”

Ruth’s eyebrows rose. “You’re going to search for Rudolf Carew’s missing suitcase of money, aren’t you?” she asked Judith.

“I might poke around a little next summer,” Judith said, blushing a little, “but only while I’m looking for Roger.”

“Lost treasure,” Ruth mused, setting aside the adventure book in her hands without glancing at it. “Untraceable cash.”

“I usually prefer to hike alone,” Judith said. “But if either of you care to accompany me . . .”

“I’m game,” Ruth told Judith. “What about you, Helma?”

“Weather permitting,” Helma said.